PENGUIN BOOKS

JUDGEMENT DAY

Penelope Lively grew up in Egypt, but settled in England after the war and took a degree in History at St Anne's College, Oxford. She is a popular children's writer and has won both the Carnegie Medal and the Whitbread Award. In 1977 she started to write for adults, with immediate success. *The Road to Lichfield* was short-listed for the 1977 Booker Prize. This was followed by *Nothing Missing but the Samovar*, a collection of short stories which won the Southern Arts Literature Award in 1978, and *Treasures of Time*, for which she received the first National Book Award for fiction. She is the author of *Next to Nature, Art, Perfect Happiness* and *According to Mark*, which was shortlisted for the 1984 Booker Prize, and *Pack of Cards*, a collection of short stories. *Moon Tiger*, her latest novel, won the 1987 Booker Prize and was shortlisted for the Whitbread Award. Many of her books are published by Penguin.

She is married to Professor Jack Lively, has a daughter and a son, and lives in Oxfordshire and London.

Penelope Lively

Judgement Day

Penguin Books

PENGUIN BOOKS

Published by the Penguin Group
27 Wrights Lane, London W8 5TZ, England
Viking Penguin Inc., 40 West 23rd Street, New York, New York 10010, USA
Penguin Books Australia Ltd, Ringwood, Victoria, Australia
Penguin Books Canada Ltd, 2801 John Street, Markham, Ontario, Canada L3R 1B4
Penguin Books (NZ) Ltd, 182–190 Wairau Road, Auckland 10, New Zealand

Penguin Books Ltd, Registered Offices: Harmondsworth, Middlesex, England

First published by William Heinemann Ltd 1980
Published in Penguin Books 1982
7 9 10 8

Printed and bound in Great Britain by
Cox & Wyman Ltd, Reading

To Jill

Chapter One

First of all, the place.

Laddenham. A village long detached from its origins, dormitory satellite of an expanding country town known for light engineering, London overspill and an intractable traffic problem. Its name hitches it still to a past. That, and a few buildings lingering here and there amid Wates and McAlpine estates, bulbous thirties semis, Victorian terraced cottages and seventies 'Executive Home' developments. A muddled place – its associations incoherent, its strata confused. Ugly for the most part, but shot here and there with grace: an avenue of old limes, a Georgian house in the High Street, a cottage-lined alley offering a slice of blue-distanced landscape. The church.

The church. St Peter and St Paul. Perilously sited, nowadays, beside the Amoco garage, its grey stone extinguished by lime green and tangerine plastic bunting flapping along the perimeter of the adjoining forecourt. On the other side, the George and Dragon's car park presses up tight against the churchyard wall. Cigarette packets and crumpled crisp bags twinkle in the long grass around the gravestones. The effect of this juxtaposition is that what must once have seemed so large, so solid, so impregnable, now squats small and a little apologetic: a pleasing anachronism, of architectural interest. Time has juggled the order of things.

The church's own chronological confusion, of course, is

absolute. Airy Dec. east window, sterner Perp. to right and left, Victorian stained glass, Norman tympanum over the west door – uncouthly carved whale and Jonah from an age when symbolism came in pictures not in words.

In a literate age, the symbolisms are more obscure. The Doom over the crossing arch, for instance, the fourteenth century wall-painting that is the church's glory and surprise, puzzles members of the congregation today. Those queerly bundled figures on one side, their form barely discernible (the plasterwork has not been restored), those other grey statuesque forms sitting up in, apparently, bathtubs. Those red monkeyish things with – toasting forks, could it be? Angels to the left, sinister and spectral figures to the right; a rising or a falling; a golden glow (despite the faded pigments) or a dark writhing obscurity. In any case, the whole thing is very difficult to make out and perhaps uncomfortable if studied in detail.

George Radwell, the vicar, coming into the church on a June morning, was surprised to see a woman standing in the nave staring intently at the painting. A tall bony young woman with stringy brown hair wearing jeans and a cotton jersey, a stranger, he thought, no one local, until she turned and glanced at him and he recognized the thin face and large mouth of the new woman next door, the one with the white mini and two children and a husband said to be something important at United Electronics. She stood there in a shaft of sunlight, bathed in gold like a stained glass Virgin, bared her teeth at him in, apparently, greeting, and turned back at once to the painting.

He cleared his throat. 'Ah,' he said, 'you must be, er . . .' and she paid him no attention at all. He was dismissed.

Clare Paling saw a sandy-haired man hovering at the doorway, a man of forty odd with the papery red skin of the very fair, blinking and shuffling and somehow inspiring distaste even at that range and on a translucent summer morning. Oh lor, she thought, the vicar of course, him from next door, and sweetly beamed before returning to the painting.

George took four steps left to the font and fiddled with the cover. Mrs Paling continued to study the Doom. He went over to the organ and shuffled the pile of sheet music. Then he marched down the nave and launched into conversation. Disastrous, as it was to turn out, conversation.

Ah, he said, you must be Mrs Paling, my churchwarden mentioned, Sydney Porter, lives in the corner house, possibly you've come across, also I've noticed the car, nice to have children around, not that I've been twitching the lace curtains, don't think. He laughed; the silly, snorty laugh that always came when he was least sure of himself. Settled in all right, I hope, he continued, very friendly place Laddenham, quite a bit going on one way and another, madrigal society meet at, er, flourishing adult whatsit I'm told, cricket if your husband plays, thought he looked as if possibly, anyway sure you'll find plenty, lot of redecorating I expect, these big Edwardian houses, vicarage badly in need of, know the area already perhaps?

And she ignored all this, not even looking at him most of the time, engrossed still by the Doom.

'Fourteenth century, I suppose,' she said. 'It's very like the one at North Leigh, isn't it? Same hand, I wonder? And the Weighing of Souls at South Leigh. The colours are remarkable.'

George mumbled something. Said he always found it a bit depressing. Made or tried to make a joke about red devils that she didn't follow. Aeroplanes? she said, staring, sorry I don't quite . . . R.A.F. base, he persisted, Willerton, ten twelve miles away, aerobatic stuff. Ah, she said, really? Moving off now to examine the screen, putting out a thin hand with long clean unpainted fingernails to touch for a moment the wooden foliage, the worn gilding of the tracery.

He drifted after her to the font, saying things. Once she turned to him and bared her teeth once more; a conversational response, it seemed to be. He could see very thin pointed breasts nudging at her jersey when she squatted down to examine the carvings.

3

She said, 'Splendid Tree of Life. I say, I do like that. Apostles. Christ in Majesty. The Lamb. What's this? Oh, it must be the Annunciation. Rather knocked about – Cromwell, I suppose. Twelfth century, Pevsner thinks. Very nice too.' She stood up.

George regarded the font. It was old, Miss Bellingham said. Miss Bellingham went on about carvings and things, a bit like this woman. Otherwise this woman wasn't like Miss Bellingham at all, who was treasurer of the Parochial Church Council and something of a busybody and had a face like the back of a bus. Mrs Paling wasn't pretty at all, but she was . . .

She made you think about sex, not to put too fine a point on it. 'Pevsner?' said George. 'Can't for the moment place . . . Yes, twelfth century, that's right.' He continued to regard the font with his head slightly on one side and the assessing expression of a person in an art gallery. It didn't feel right; a church isn't an art gallery; he had never looked at the font like that before.

Mrs Paling gave him the toothy grin again. 'Never mind. Well, I must go.' She headed for the door; he was dismissed once more.

He beat her to the door, opened it. 'So glad we've met at last. Must come in for a glass of, er. And look, don't let the children keep you from the Sunday service, we welcome children, everyone brings them, babies and all, fearful racket sometimes.' The snorty laugh.

She stared at him. 'Oh,' she said, 'we shan't be coming to services. We're agnostics. Thanks all the same.'

George went scarlet. R.C. he could have dealt with, non-comformist or whatever. Other creeds, no problem – you nodded understandingly, implying breadth and tolerance. Or people who weren't anything, for that matter; you evaded their own evading eye and talked about something else. But such an outright statement of unbelief knocked you sideways. It was provocative, unnecessary.

He snorted. Waved over her shoulder to a passer-by to

indicate ease and failure to be disconcerted. Felt in his pocket for the cigarettes he gave up five years ago. Said loudly, too loudly 'Quite, quite. Well, in that case. Naturally, though, one assumed, seeing you in the church, and interested' – he waved at the font, the Doom, the screen – 'interested in all that, well of course one supposed C. of E.'

'Interest in ecclesiastical architecture,' said Mrs Paling sweetly, 'is not restricted to Christians. And infrequent amongst them, I've noticed.'

She was paying him attention now. As much attention as the church furnishings. Almost. She doesn't like me, George thought, she doesn't like me and she doesn't think I matter much. He was in a lather of emotion; resentment and obstinacy and a whole lot else. She had this horsy face and large teeth and long thin thighs and a very small behind. Not a pretty woman, oh no.

He crashed on, his voice coming out shrill now, hectoring. 'What I want to know with you people is – what about when you're dead? Then what?'

Mrs Paling gazed at him. 'Then nothing, I've always assumed.'

'Where d'you think you'll go, that's what I want to know?'

'Do you mean', said Mrs Paling, 'will I be wanting a bit of the churchyard? No thanks.' She began, again, to depart.

'Death,' George insisted, beetroot now to the hairline, 'is the problem.'

'Oh no it isn't,' said Mrs Paling. 'It's life that's the problem. That's where you people go wrong. Sorry. No point in discussion really. Always ends up stalemate' – teeth gleaming at him again – 'Must go now, ought to be in Spelbury. I like your church. Bye.'

And that, for the time being, was that.

*   *   *

George Radwell had entered the Church because of a typing mistake. Or rather the mistake triggered the process that had sent him, eventually, into St Stephen's Hall. A secretary, in the list briefing the Headmaster of his school on the career intentions of the sixth form leavers, had substituted 'Theological' for 'Technical'. 'Theological college?' read the Headmaster in surprise, looking with new eyes at the ginger-haired boy whose name he never could recall, whose school career was so undistinguished as to leave him totally anonymous, without even transgressions by which to be remembered. 'That's interesting, er, Radwell, now what made you plump for the ministry? I don't think we've had anyone going into the Church for some while. How interesting. We must have a talk about the various colleges – personally I've always thought well of Loxfield though of course St Chad's is highly regarded.' And on he went, talking now of vocations and deploring, discreetly, the decision of Manners, the Captain of Cricket, to go in for estate agency; until at last he came to a halt and George, crimson and desperate, was able to mumble that actually there was a mistake, that actually . . .

The Headmaster stared at him. 'The tech,' he said, 'I see. The tech.' He wrote something on a pad; he was no longer engaged. No longer was a man of substance and discrimination finding George interesting, a matter for concern. 'Very well, Radwell. Have a word with the Careers Master if there's anything you want to know. Would you ask Tremlett to come in now, please.'

George went home, humiliated. On the way, he thought about the Church; he thought vaguely of carols at Christmas, of the Hallelujah Chorus and Salisbury Cathedral, of forceful manly clerics on television discussion programmes. He had nothing against Christianity, he realized, nothing at all. That evening, he told his mother of the incident with the Headmaster, of the mistake. His father had died when he was fifteen. Mrs Radwell, for whom little that he did was right, for whom carping at him had become an occupation, was silenced for once. She didn't laugh. She reversed her knitting and started on another row. Halfway along the row she said, 'You could have done worse. There's some lovely houses, vicarages, for a family. It's a nice sort of job.'

Later that week, George went to see the local priest. He was given a glass of sherry and talked to for an hour and more; he stayed for lunch; the man's wife called him 'dear' and later he found himself giving them a hand with some gardening chores. They seemed, to his surprise, to like him.

At the end of term he asked to see the Headmaster again.

He had been worried, before arrival at college, by his lack of either faith or calling, until it dawned on him that those, after all, were what presumably the course was designed to supply. Which indeed it did, more or less. He quite enjoyed it. Whereas at school he had been among the proletariat of the dim, the featureless, the unassertive, here he bloomed a little. There were others with greater inadequacies than his. By his second year he had found a small talent for debate, been elected secretary of the Junior Common Room and played snooker for the college against a rival establishment. He had also got drunk twice and put his hand inside the shirt of a friend's sister. More importantly, he was bolstered by being a part of something larger than himself; he was no longer alone with his failings.

He spent several years as a curate in north London, where he found himself out of depth, made to feel a lack-lustre figure both by his more racy colleagues and the parishioners. He was no good at Youth Clubs and disturbed black teenagers. They made rings round him, as did the jaunty young vicar and his jeaned, chain-smoking wife and her brisk emphatic community worker friends. When the Laddenham living came up he fled with relief.

*   *   *

The church, the Amoco garage and the George and Dragon's car park face what was once the nucleus of Laddenham, the village green, and is now a grassy area called the Green, with bus shelter, a few flowerbeds and a seat for the elderly provided

7

by the British Legion In Memory of The Fallen. There are also some fine pink-flowered chestnuts and a small play area for young children with revolving wooden contraptions and some swings. The area itself is a triangle, the two long sides formed by rows of houses confronting each other through the chestnuts: a set of large Edwardian villas including the vicarage and the Palings' house, and a line of three and four bedroomed houses built in the sixties on the site of a condemned nineteenth century terrace. The Edwardian houses, which rarely come on the market and are the most highly priced in Laddenham when they do, have large gardens with brick walls and too much privet and laburnum. The modern houses, also expensive, have shaven lawns fore and aft, standard roses and small weeping willows. The area is considered the most desirable part of Laddenham, being quiet, free of council housing, and within easy walk of the shops and schools.

Sydney Porter, churchwarden and retired accountant, came out of his house to sweep his doorstep and saw the vicar in the church porch talking to the new woman from number five. He looked away at once, in case either of them should see him, not to get involved, and when he had shaken the mat and done the step and closed the front gate left open as usual by the milkman the woman was gone and the vicar was standing there in the sun, alone. He went on standing there and Sydney, whose day was already apportioned, as was each of his days, went indoors, a small, spare, neat man, nearer seventy than sixty, accustomed to solitude.

Sydney's house stood at the end of the row of modern ones, on the corner by the church. It was, however, an uneasy juxtaposition since Sydney's was not reconstituted stone with double garage and playroom/granny annexe but a bow-windowed brick building with something vaguely marine about its lines, slipped in next to the old terrace in the thirties and no doubt an enviable property then but now much over-shadowed by the new houses and the revived prosperity of the Edwardian villas.

Sydney had had to endure the demolition of the condemned terrace and the building of the new houses, twelve years earlier. He had lived through it grim faced and uncomplaining, dusting daily instead of twice a week, polishing and re-polishing the procession of brass elephants in the hall, flapping and realigning the gardening magazines that lay on the lounge table. Stoically, week by week, he had gathered up and burned the rubbish that drifted from the building site onto his garden. On the night after the bulldozers had moved in he had woken shouting from a nightmare, and had gone to the window to see, in the moonlight, the shattered windowless shells of the few remaining cottages. In the morning, at the office where he then worked, they had been surprised to see him shaking. He wasn't, you'd have thought, a nervy man; a bit close, perhaps, but not nervy. He'd been away for a week or so after that, flu or something, people said, and thereafter appeared his usual self, quiet, composed, reserved.

The new houses rose from the rubble of the old. The raw earth of their fenced gardens sent forth lawns and paving from the Garden Centre and neatly spaced and labelled shrubs and, in summer, padded and canopied seats and hoses with sprinkler attachments. Sydney got to know their occupants by name: the Marshalls and the Haddows and the Coggans.

And the Bryans, next door. Keith and Shirley. And the child, Martin.

The Bryans did not have a lawn with a sprinkler, or labelled shrubs. Their garden plot remained much as the builders had left it: things seeded themselves and grew haphazardly, rank clumps of grass, groundsel and chickweed. The boy played in it, alone. From time to time someone planted lobelia or african marigolds, forgot to weed or water, and the flowers shrivelled or were smothered.

Sydney Porter, his morning already planned – hoe the seed-beds, cut the grass, tie back the climber if time – came out of the house and went over to the potting-shed. There, he selected a hoe from the row of garden tools. The tools, blades

9

and tines wiped clean of earth, hung in gradation on the wall, orchestrated from long-handled fruit-tree pruners to wooden bulb dibber. Flower-pots were stacked in columns; hanks of twine were ranged on hooks; sprays and fertilizers were lined up on a shelf. Sydney went over to the vegetable plot and set to work.

'I can never see what people get out of gardening. You're always at it, Mr Porter, aren't you?'

She seemed to be forever yawning, Shirley Bryan. Yawning and scratching an armpit. She stood at the fence now, doing just that, a fluffy-haired girl with a bad complexion.

Sydney paused. He thought. Eventually he said, 'It's having control over something, I suppose. Knowing what will happen.'

'If I try to grow things they just flop over and die, or something eats them. You can't win.'

'You get the odd bother,' said Sydney smoothly, 'not enough to put you off altogether.' He went back to the hoeing: thrust and back, just deep enough to clip the seedling weeds, a wake of tiny wilting shoots behind him, French beans pushing up nicely to right and left. Shirley Bryan continued to watch, arms akimbo along the top of the fence.

'Keith's got his promotion.'

'Very nice.'

He wished she'd go away.

'Five hundred and a Granada at the end of the year.'

'Ah.'

'Not that much of it'll come my way, I daresay.' She yawned again. 'Hey, there's Martin's ball under that bush of yours. He was on about what had happened to that last night. D'you mind chucking it over, Mr Porter. Thanks a lot.'

The boy, over the years, had left infancy behind, topped the garden fence, acquired footballs and guns. He was a thin, pale-faced child, quiet, to Sydney's relief. Quiet and rather solitary, playing mostly by himself, strange furtive games along the fence and among the bushes and saplings that, eventually, had grown and furnished the end of the Bryans' garden.

He did not play with the Coggan children, next door on the other side, the two tidy, fair-haired little girls. Neither did the Bryans consort much with the Coggans, Sue and John. John Coggan of E. J. Coggan & Son, Estate Agents, 14 High Street, Laddenham. A different type of family, Sydney could see, more homely people, the garden spruce, Sue Coggan regular as clockwork trundling her pushchair along to the shops, in later years hurrying the girls to school, off to collect them at three-thirty.

Martin Bryan took himself to school, brought himself home.

John Coggan sat on the Parish Council and was chairman of the Parent Teacher Association. A stocky, brown-haired man, running to fat a little, nicely paired with Sue, so small and trim and fresh-faced beneath her shiny fair fringe.

The Coggans, all four, attended matins every Sunday; the Bryans, never.

The Bryans, the Coggans, Sydney Porter, George Radwell – for all these people Laddenham had come to seem a satisfactory choice. A nice locality, Sue Coggan thought, a lovely house, plenty of children for the girls to play with. Five miles from the motorway, Keith Bryan would say, two hours dead to Piccadilly. George Radwell found it a great deal pleasanter than north London. Not being a thoughtful man, he had never dwelt on the slippery nature of choice in human affairs; he felt that he had chosen Laddenham, just as he had come to feel that he had chosen to go into the Church.

Sydney Porter, who had long since ceased to take much interest in questions of choice or blind accident, simply moved through the days, doing what had to be done. He quite liked Laddenham; it was as good a place as any. You had to feed up the soil a bit, but there was no clay. Things went on the same, on the whole, year in, year out. The odd fuss about a planning permission or a road scheme, but nothing to disturb, really. Hardly ever.

11

Just sometimes, nowadays, the motor-bikes. Roaring through the Green, always after dark, deep into the night, a gang of them, shattering the quiet like an explosion, the more violent because unexpected. The first time the din had had him half out of bed, wrenched from sleep, his heart thumping. And then they were gone so quickly he thought he might even have dreamed the sound. But they'd been back a week later, circling the Green two or three times.

Thus the place, the people. In random association.

Chapter Two

I have no friends, said Clare Paling to the bathroom ceiling. I am married to a man who is sweeping all before him in the electronics industry and I have no friends. I live in a big expensive house that would be the envy of many. I am a crack cook. My husband's success is such that it keeps him from home five and a half days out of seven and ten hours out of twenty-four. I am well educated, considered good-looking, an experienced driver and I have no friends. I don't have a lover either.

Downstairs, the house rocked to the din of sibling warfare. Clare turned the hot tap on.

I have a new white mini and the most expensive brand of dishwasher on the market. I can read Anglo-Saxon, speak French, respond to metaphysical poetry and I have no friends. I have no friends because all the people I used to know live somewhere else and I am somewhat off-putting in manner. I off-put by speaking sharply and smiling too expansively. When I am getting bored I show my teeth. I've seen, in mirrors. I grin and grin and there are my teeth, large and looking more yellow than they really are.

Downstairs, a television exploded into sound.

I have a happy marriage and a father who is a big wheel at the Treasury. When I look at my children I know that they are the most wonderful creatures I have ever seen and I do not know whether to exult or to weep. I read books and the world appals me. Sometimes I wake in the night and shiver. And then I walk out into the beauty of it and I am amazed. All my life I have wondered how we endure it as we do, knowing what we know.

Sometimes I feel so charged with energy that I think I might burst out of my skin. Walking across the recreation ground I know that I could go on for ever without stopping, without ever tiring, could walk off the face of the earth. They should use people like me to power industries. Solve the energy crisis just like that.

She turned the tap on again. Sang. In a deep voice, not bad sounding. Excerpts from *Carmen*.

*   *   *

Sue Coggan, a hundred and ten yards away, washed the tea things and thought: if we have another next year, when Tracy's just turned six, October would be best, well after the summer holidays and before Christmas, so I'd be up and about in good time for the shopping. Three's a nice number – two girls and a little boy – touch wood, cross fingers. She dried the dishes and took her diary from the kitchen shelf. We ought to start it in January, in that case. The diary for this year showed January of next as a series of black lines, one for each week. In the second was pencilled 'Car for 6,000 mile service' and in the third 'Holiday bookings. Dad's birthday.' Sue took a biro, hesitated, made a cryptic red asterisk in the first week. The christening on Boxing Day, she thought, nice, when the parents are here, and I'll have a new winter coat, one of those full-backed ones, in a light tweed. And the girls in little matching dresses.

She went to the window and saw Martin Bryan outside on the pavement. Lurking behind the low brick wall, his head surfacing above it every now and then. Playing something. Not watching telly like any other child would be at this point in the day. A sad sort of kid really, but what could you expect, parents like that? Sue frowned to herself and shook her head,

14

thinking of Shirley Bryan – such a slut, and forever on the borrow – out of this, out of that, can I scrounge half a loaf, a cup of sugar, forgot to go to the shops. Mucky house. Keith Bryan fiddling his expenses without a doubt, all those jazzy clothes, the two of them off out to the roadhouse on Saturday nights and Martin left alone in the house as like as not, maybe one shouldn't be turning a blind eye, but what could you do?

* * *

Count ten and then look over the wall again. If it's all clear, sprint up the path. Head down in case they fire from the window. Eight, nine, ten. They're looking. Down again. Keep crouched, they may shoot, they may . . .

I'm cold, he thought. He had no jersey on. He didn't know where the jersey was, couldn't be bothered to look for it. He didn't know where Mum was, either. She'd left bread and peanut butter for tea on the kitchen table and a note saying back later. Probably she'd gone to the pictures in Spelbury. The telly wouldn't work again, she'd forgotten to get the man to come. That meant they'd go out tonight to the pub. They couldn't sit in if there was no telly.

He peeked over the wall again. She'd seen him now, Mrs Coggan, she was frowning at him and shaking her head. He'd better go. It was raining, anyway. He'd have liked to watch their telly, it would be 'Extraordinary'; but that would mean asking, and he couldn't.

* * *

Keith Bryan, phoning home to say he'd be late (bit of a hassle over an order gone astray, have to stay on and do some paperwork), let it ring ten times and thought, well, blow that, she can't say I didn't try. He felt a bit let down – the story all lined up and then no one to tell it to. He put on his jacket and went downstairs two at a time and into the car park.

He felt better, with the Capri round him, driving into the heavy traffic on the by-pass, nosing at the tail-lights of some

15

silly bugger in an old Morris who thought he could cope with the fast lane. That was more like it; that was how to sort out the sheep from the goats. The headlights swept the dark road; John Travolta snarled away about love on Radio One; he'd have liked to go on like this for hours, not just the five mingy miles to the Green Man. The Green Man where Mrs Comstock of Barrow and Co., Debbie Comstock, her with the blonde hair and throaty voice, would be waiting to have a talk over a drink about that joint marketing project. Very nice too. He began to sing along with John Travolta. For a few minutes you could forget the boundaries: the eight thousand a year and fringe benefits; the three-bedroom twenty-six thousand five hundred detached with double garage. Shirley. Himself. You were up, up and away. Ten feet tall. A man could breathe.

* * *

The Parochial Church Council, gathered round the vicarage dining-room table, had read and digested the Diocesan Architect's report. They were in the process, now, of taking in the full implications of the estimate presented by the firm of church restoration experts recommended by the Diocesan Architect. George Radwell, bemused, had wondered at first if the figures were a bit wild; could all those noughts be correct? Even Sydney Porter, despite his profession, had been taken aback. But Jim Squires, brother to Squires the builder, had said yes, they would be, it's the scaffolding, see, the labour, and all that lead, and the guttering, and this rot in the vestry, and the pinning above the porch. It's not tuppence, nowadays, all that. Miss Bellingham had sighed and tutted and said everything was so dear, only last week she'd had a bill for fifty-seven pounds from the garage. Fifty-seven pounds, I ask you!

The church, seen through the vicarage window, looked solid enough, hunched there in the dusk, though dwarfed, admittedly, by the wall of the car park and the two storey block of luxury flats behind the Amoco garage. Smaller, perhaps than once it had been – or seemed to be – but enduring

16

enough, surely? This catalogue of ills was somehow indecent, this chronicle of decay and disease and infirmity, as though some reticent old lady had foisted on you chapter and verse of her medical history. The Parochial Church Council, in flight from the problems that lay on the table before them, this dizzying sheaf of figures and prognostications, gazed out of the window and confronted the situation each according to his or her own lights.

Miss Bellingham thought new altar cloths would be an idea while they were about it, and the floor polisher was on its last legs.

Sydney Porter wondered if you could perhaps get the total down a bit by bringing in a local firm, at least for the more straightforward work. Jim Squires – his brother in mind – nodded sagely.

Mrs Harrison said briskly that of course the Mothers' Union would have a Jumble Sale, several if necessary. And the Fête proceeds could be diverted from the Christian Aid Fund.

George thought about fifty thousand pounds. The figure printed itself on the window, with curlicues and loops and squiggles like the majestic script on old five pound notes, the big white ones. Through the phantom script he saw the black of the road, shiny in rain, the fresh green of the willow in the Coggans' garden, the golden fabric of St Peter and St Paul, crouched there in reduced circumstances. He saw Mr Paling's car go by, slowing down to turn into his garage. The sight of this brought Mrs Paling to mind: she floated into the centre panel of the window and hung there like, and yet most unlike, the Virgin in the north window of the church. She hung there, grinning, and then, most deliberately, removed her blouse.

'. . . some sort of anniversary celebration,' said Miss Bellingham. And then, more sharply, 'What do you think, Vicar?' The Parochial Church Council sat in expectation, looking at George, while George stared at the window in which Mrs Paling, grinning still, had begun to dissolve until there was nothing to be seen but her teeth, like the Cheshire Cat. 'Quite,' he said. 'I was just about to suggest it myself, I'm entirely with you.'

*　　*　　*

'Are you joking?' said Clare Paling. She looked at her husband across the kitchen table, over the remains of pigeon casserole and a not bad bottle of plonk from the supermarket. 'No, you're not, I see. What do you propose? Shall I run for presidency of the Women's Institute?'

Peter Paling, at thirty-five, had a receding hairline. It had begun its recession in his late twenties and had been the subject of a running joke between Clare and Peter, to do with those uncertain fellows in London tube advertisements, restored to confidence and potency by a nifty grafting job. Peter, lacking neither, would live with his increasing scalp exposure and indeed subtly turn it to his advantage. He was one of these men who look not exactly older than their years but as though they have profited from them rather more than most; a youngish man with the substance of an older one.

He was recommending to his wife that she take part in local activities. He had also mentioned, in passing, that a new European connection of the firm's would mean he had to spend several days a month in Brussels.

'I daresay you've got a point', Clare went on amiably. 'I need occupation. The local schools are fully staffed, so there are no openings for me there. Since I am no good with my needle I am not likely to start the cottage industry that will become the Laura Ashley of the nineteen nineties. I can't stand dogs or horses so it's no good trying to crash county circles. I am totally unathletic. Gardening appals me. So you think I should take up good works?'

She had given up her publishing job when they moved to Laddenham. Do you mind? he had said guiltily, standing there with the letter in his hand, the letter propelling him several rungs up a ladder. The countryside's quite pretty, I'm told, are

18

you sure you won't mind? And she had answered, truthfully as it happened, that she didn't. I am not, she had said, you must realize, particularly ambitious. Industrious, in my way, yes; ambitious, no. You will have to take on the ambition part, you're better at it. No, I don't mind. I shall be perfectly happy reading books I want to read instead of those I have to read. A period of tranquil reflection will do me no harm at all.

She had seen it coming. In the early days of their marriage, the delectable time in London and on the European tour, she had known that this wouldn't last. Promising young men, destined for ultimate stardom, must spend a period in the thick of things, not in air-conditioned city centre offices but where the objects for distribution are actually made. Light industry is mainly situated well outside London, in expanding and usually – for that reason, no doubt – unappealing towns. The Laddenham job had come as no surprise.

He filled her glass.

'I thought we were only drinking half. We shall have hangovers.'

'A little dangerous living might be a good thing.'

'All living,' said Clare, 'is dangerous.'

'You, my love, are a fatalist. You spend your life expecting the worst.'

'A hostage to fortune.'

'It's all this reading. You'll do your eyes in, apart from anything else. Are those the new glasses?'

'Do you like them?'

'They're sexy,' said Peter, 'in a peculiar way.'

'Oh, good. You think books foster pessimism, then?'

'Well,' he said cautiously, 'I've never gone in for them on your scale, so my judgement might lack bite, but on the whole I've always found real life a lot more prosaic.'

'Are we talking about fact or fiction?'

'Novels,' said Peter, 'always pose situations which are either extreme or telescope time, as it were. Life mostly isn't like that.'

'True, up to a point. They are supposed to tell a story, of course.'

'History, on the other hand, which I find all over the house these days, is full of disaster but large tracts of it, for many people, are really quite uneventful.'

'Oh quite. In fact most of us aren't even conscious that it's going on. By the way I wish you wouldn't keep moving *Human Documents of the Industrial Revolution* off the shelf by the cooker. It's there for when I'm involved with tedious stirring operations.'

'Ah,' he said, 'I'm sorry. I quite like the glasses, but do you have to keep them on, I thought they were for reading?'

'I was looking at the wine bottle label. They can come off now.'

'It hardly bears that close inspection.'

'I was wondering what the picture of the man stamping was. Treading grapes I suppose. Not that one imagines these were ever trod. But to get back to what we started with – you think charitable enterprises would be a good idea?'

'There must be something that needs interfering with. The school?'

'I am not,' said Clare with dignity, 'intending a career of interference. And in any case the Parent Teacher Association is in the hands of a cabal comprising that estate agent opposite and various cronies. They don't like me. I alarm their wives and they don't care for my tone of voice. No chance of a *coup d'état* there. Besides, there'd be no joy in it. It's a perfectly good school, all one could do is raise money for the minibus fund. No standing at the gates with a placard demanding educational justice. Sorry – have to think again.'

'Perhaps it's not really a problem,' he suggested, 'since you say you're perfectly happy.'

'I never said any such thing. Who ever experienced perfect happiness? Certainly not me. Not with my temperament, but I'm as happy as I would ever expect to be, and grateful with it.'

'That's all right,' said Peter. 'Don't mention it.'

'Not to you, you nit. To something altogether more metaphysical.'

'Nevertheless, I think local involvement might be no bad thing.'

'Putting down some roots?'

He began to grind coffee. 'You've always rather dug yourself into places before. What about something else, then? A course at the local university?'

'No thanks. I've had quite enough education already, goodness knows what any more would lead to. No, that won't do. We shall have to give the matter some serious thought. You may well be right. And now tell me about this Brussels thing.'

*　　*　　*

Sydney Porter said goodnight to the other members of the Parochial Church Council outside the vicarage and crossed the Green to his house. Passing the church, he paused for a moment to look at it, thinking both of its ailments and its antiquity. He had been surprised to learn of its age. Sydney was not very strong on history, he knew; doing a sum in his head he reckoned the foundation of the church as not long after 1066, a date that was familiar. Well, given that, it stood to reason that it wouldn't be in very good shape, structurally. Though only bits of it were from then, of course, most of it was much newer. Funny how you never really gave a lot of thought to how long a place had been there; you acted as sidesman, Sunday after Sunday, saw to the hymn books, locked up on alternate nights, without ever really thinking about that.

The church on the corner of Mansell Road had been big and black, not like this at all, a big black London church. It had dwarfed the houses, rather than the other way about. Coming back that morning in 1941 it had been the only solid thing left, standing foursquare alongside the row of blasted shells. Only later, going in, had he seen the wreckage within, the floor and seats white with fallen plaster, the chancel open to the sky, the altar a mess of splintered wood and rubble. He had stood there a long time, alone; outside the rescue squads were working still, their boots crunching on broken glass.

They were going to be hard put to it to raise all that cash; and the vicar not a go-ahead sort of man, either. A long haul, it would be. Not that there wasn't money about, you only had to look around you to see that. But not much of it would come the way of the restoration fund, Sydney suspected. He let himself into the house and went into the kitchen to make a cup of tea. Tea and a biscuit, and the television news, and see what was on after, and an early night if it wasn't up to much. He stood at the window while the kettle boiled; dark now and lights at windows around the Green, discreet glowing curtained squares, except the big house by the vicarage where they were bright and bare so that you could see clean into the rooms, a man and woman in one, a kitchen, sitting at a table with glasses in their hands. Those new people. I've got good eye-sight, Sydney thought, man of my age, good as when I was in the Navy, all but; he drew his own curtains and went through into the lounge.

He sat in the chintz-covered chair that had once been in the Mansell Road house while information was expertly and ex-pensively conveyed to him: an assessment of the political situation in Namibia, a run-down on Britain's position vis-a-vis the European monetary fund, a consideration of an impending industrial dispute (opposing points of view dis-creetly outlined). Sydney drank tea and wondered about switching to round pod French beans this year. On the screen, there was talk now of distresses in some far off place; fleeing figures in a street, a man crouching with a rifle. A child crying. Sydney watched and sighed, stirred by the recollection of feeling, rather than feeling itself. Poor wretches. His ghost walked among them, outraged by the world. But none of this could touch him now; lightning does not strike twice, and in any case there was nothing left for it to strike.

Football results rolled up, and the weather. Nothing worth watching after. Sydney switched off and prepared to go to bed.

*   *   *

Next door, Keith Bryan also watched the news. The row he'd had with Shirley about forgetting to phone the TV repair man had petered out when he discovered that in fact it was only the plug that was faulty. Just as well, in the event, or there'd have been a hefty charge for damn all. Now, he sprawled apathetic in front of the set. At one point he was aroused and annoyed by the discovery that power workers pull in over a hundred a week. He also noted the make of car used by the chairman of British Rail, and a sexy air hostess behind the right shoulder of a departing American politician. When the newsreader started talking about unemployment figures he went out to the kitchen for a beer. There, he caught sight of himself for an instant in the mirror by the door – a shortish fellow with round shoulders reaching into the fridge for a can of Pale Ale. And knew with a spurt of anger that there was some mistake. Keith Bryan was somewhere else – a bullish bronzed black-haired chap in a cricket sweater, with a buttery blonde in tow, drinking shorts at a bar aglow with horse brasses and copper pans. He went back to the sitting-room. 'Don't ask me if I want one, will you?' said Shirley. He flung himself back into his chair without looking at her. On the television screen, people shot each other in the streets of some American city; in fantasy, not fact, as he recognized from the excitable camera work and the non-chalance of the protagonists. 'Shut up,' he said, 'I'm following this series.'

Chapter Three

The school, Laddenham primary, was seven minutes adult walk from the Green and various distances where children were concerned, according to age. The Coggan girls, accompanied each way by their mother, took between eight and ten minutes. Martin Bryan, when late, could do it in four and a half, running, or anything up to an hour otherwise, going by the churchyard and through the gap in the car park wall and over the building site, or dawdling along the High Street with a stop off at the sweet shop. The Paling children, Anna and Thomas, could also extend the journey almost indefinitely, if unaccompanied; when driven by their mother in the white mini it was three and a half minutes dead, door to door.

Martin Bryan and the Coggans went to the primary school because that was where children went to school. The Palings went there because Clare and Peter, who had opinions about education, and knew a thing or two, had observed that a good state primary school is as good as anything provided by the private sector and free into the bargain. The Coggan girls and Anna Paling did not consort out of school hours because Anna thought Tracy and Mandy silly. Thomas and Martin did not consort partly because Martin was two and a half years older than Thomas, thus laying on him the onus of any overtures that might be made, and partly because Thomas had once seen

Martin crying in the school lavatory and had been intolerably embarrassed. In any case, Martin did not consort much with anyone. If they found themselves returning to the Green at the same time, they walked separately, or on opposite sides of the street. But then, so did the two Palings, who had proper ideas about indifference to one's sibling when released from the conventions of the home.

The school was bright and airy and a credit to the system. The walls were covered with eye-catching examples of child art-work; witches and dragons vied with the life-cycle of the frog and what people wore in Elizabethan times, in cheerful evidence that the life of the imagination was not despised in these parts. The teachers tended to be young; some were male and bearded. The children gave every indication of well-being; the place buzzed with activity and the early morning influx showed no sign of reluctance. The school dinners were ample and nutritious.

Not many of the children had a speech that could at once be recognized as of the place: just a few. The Laddenham voice, subtly distinct from the Midlands but not yet opening out into the fullness of Gloucestershire and parts west, was confined to those few whose family names might have been found on the tombstones in the churchyard of St Peter and St Paul, and, in some cases, not even to them. Most children spoke the unplaceable and even classless English of radio and television performers; the language they used had the same ubiquity. Only occasionally (the Opies would have been gratified) did a childish code word surface that was entirely local in origin: a word for truce, the dialect of scatology, an insult. The Paling children, within a matter of weeks and barely conscious that they were doing so, had learned to temper their accents, slip into a more anonymous pronunciation, and call things by the right names. At home, they reverted to their usual style, so that for many months their parents were unaware of this chameleon dexterity, until one day Clare, waiting outside the school playground, heard with amazement her son shouting in

25

an alien tongue. She had the tact not to comment, but thought about the matter. It struck her as curious that the ability – willingness, perhaps – to accept the requirements of a place should come so much more readily to children. One could look at it in two lights, of course: it could seem a sheep-like conformity, or alternatively a refreshing knack of discarding old habits. Either way, it was as though the spirit of place, nowadays, exerted its power only over the young.

The spirit of place was in any case hard to detect in Laddenham. There was no shop or other building in the High Street whose counterpart could not have been found elsewhere: Boots, Dewhurst, Tesco; a nineteenth century ironmonger's façade, a fifties brutalist bank, an Edwardian pub. The road-signs, recently renewed and standardized, pointed you to out-lying hamlets in lettering that suggested cities the size of Birmingham. The Midland Bank had a clock recording the time of day on the eastern and western coasts of the United States. Only the church and a few of the older houses were a reminder that this place lay on the limestone spine of England, and was built from its own bones. The new housing estates, rushed up to meet the boom of fifteen years ago, were in brick or a garish reconstituted stone of inflexible texture. They encircled the old village centre, the High Street, the church and the Green, their street names quaintly rural and suggesting quite another ambiance: The Grove, Willow Way, Rivermead, Swan Lane.

Nearly everyone worked in Spelbury, the thriving town of which Laddenham and other expanded villages were satellites. Spelbury made the internal organs of radios and televisions, a few selected car components, women's tights and stockings, and processed frozen foods. It was a place that had been designated for prosperity immediately after the war, a London overspill town, and had flourished accordingly: industry had come, people had come, houses had been built, and Spelbury had tripled, quadrupled in size. Only the street plan of the town centre, an elongated triangle enclosing an open space, and the Friday cattle market, remembered its ancestral function. It was still in trade, of course, but no longer trade of a local nature: pigs and sheep and cows. Nowadays, the container lorries feeding Spelbury's factories might come from Scotland, from the east coast, from the continent.

Ten miles away, R.A.F. Willerton sprawled runways and silver hangars and several acres of red brick housing for personnel across the landscape, and provided considerable extra purchasing power for the Spelbury shops, and clientele for the Saturday night discos, the pubs, and the two cinemas.

Aircraft noise split the skies, periodically. Laddenham could congratulate itself on not being beneath one of the main flight paths. On the whole, the aircraft swept north up the river valley before turning right for Europe and the Middle and Far East, or left for elsewhere. The gleaming, backswept planes were alleged by knowledgeable locals to carry nuclear bombs; others disputed this. The less sinister transport aircraft, low slung and erect-tailed, lumbered about the horizon all day long, so much a part of the scenery that a landscape painter, seeking local exactitude, would need to incorporate one, pottering above the low hills, the hedge-striped valleys, the greens and golds and fawns of the agricultural midlands.

The R.A.F. display team, the Red Devils, was based at Willerton.

The first time Clare Paling saw them was on the morning after her conversation with Peter about her occupation – or lack of it – and three days after her exchange with George Radwell in the church. She had dropped the children at school, been to Spelbury to do the week's shopping at Sainsbury's and then, on a whim, driven straight out of the town in the opposite direction to Laddenham. She had stopped the mini, presently, on a side road, at a point where the road crossed a small stream by way of an old stone bridge; a delectable riverine landscape of willows and watermeadows and buttercups. She sat on the wall of the bridge and saw flowing weed, like green hair, with little white flowers blooming just above the water, dragged this way and that by the current. It was early summer. The grass was thick, the trees in full leaf; the willows along the stream bank were a sharp yellow-green against the steel grey of a rain-cloud behind them, a miraculous effect of light and texture. And then suddenly there was a disturbance of air, a wind that sprang up from nowhere; a blackbird shrieked; a bullock cantered off with its tail up. Across the skyline, above the willows, across that pewter backcloth there swept a scarlet aeroplane, not a hundred yards away, not, it seemed, a hundred yards above the ground, a huge scarlet steel dart, quite soundless. It was there above the trees – and then gone so quickly it could have been a hallucination.

There came another, and another, and another, with only yards between them. She stood up, her hand to her mouth, amazed. And then the sound arrived: a great tearing roar, rising and falling, once, twice, three, four, five times – once for each plane.

It was astonishing. She was filled with wild exhilaration. The shock of it. The beauty of those shapes fleeing across the dark sky, the brilliance of the colour; the sudden intrusion, the sense of something quite merciless and irresistible blasting its way across the tranquil countryside. There was a hot metallic smell in the air now. And, looking away and upwards, she saw them again, but high, high up, thousands of feet up, tiny scarlet gnats flying in tight formation, making an arrow that vanished into a grey heap of cloud.

She found the whole thing intensely stimulating and drove home too fast, narrowly missing an accident, the sight of the red aeroplanes still printed on her eyeballs.

*   *   *

Sydney Porter was erecting runner bean poles when the Red Devils came over Laddenham. He did not see them but was assaulted by the noise, seconds after they had passed; it was

28

as though the whole sky raged, and he thought at first of thunder, but it was clear and bright now, with just a distant cloudbank piled up away beyond Spelbury. He stood there, looking up at the sky, and then the girl called over the fence, Shirley Bryan next door, 'Hey – did you see, Mr Porter? Those formation fliers from the R.A.F. – fantastic!' He shook his head.

She was hanging up washing, inefficiently, dropping things into the dirt and then giving them just a quick shake before pegging them out. Now she came and leaned up against the fence, chatting on about how she'd never have the patience to grow all those veg, but it must be nice, not having to go to the shops so much. 'But you're ever so methodical, aren't you? I've seen you in Tesco, with your list, ticking things off.' She giggled. 'Don't think I was spying – just I caught sight of you across the aisle. Wish I could be so organized. Keith's always on at me for the lousy housekeeper I am. Well, he could have guessed as much when he married me, frankly.' She laughed again, a laugh that Sydney found irritating, a mannerism merely. She yawned, a huge uncovered yawn so that he looked away quickly, back to the runner beans, a more engaging sight altogether. Now she was on about her husband, embarrassingly, personal comments that one would prefer not to hear; Sydney bound poles together with string and tried to think about something else. The church, this appeal, now that was a thing they'd have to give their minds to, over the next month. Fund-raising. Letters to important people, the big folk round about, the Chamber of Commerce and that. 'Toothpaste,' said Shirley Bryan, 'all over the basin. When he's spat. I tell you, I could scream sometimes. Oh well, that's marriage. You should be thankful you stayed a bachelor, Mr Porter.'

He clamped the last two poles together, wound the string and clipped off the end with his knife. Tested the line for strength: firm enough. 'I'm not a bachelor,' he said to the bean-poles. 'Not me. My wife died. Long time ago.' And heard her noises of surprise and regret and interest.

He picked his things up, the string and the knife and the spade, and stumped back towards the house, not looking at her again. Angry at being jumped into that much self-exposure. But he couldn't tell a lie, not even a lie by omission, never had been able to.

*　　*　　*

George Radwell was on the telephone to the secretary of the Parish Council about the booking of the village hall when the Red Devils went over. The noise blotted out all; he sat there mouthing, saying into the roaring air, 'Not a Saturday, we thought, a weekday we'd be likely to get more people, would next Thursday be . . .' And then the row receded and gradually Charlie Webb came through saying, 'Eh? What's that, Vicar? Can't hear you, terrible line. Just say that again, would you.'

The date fixed, he put the receiver down. Agenda. Speakers. Me, I suppose. The Diocesan Architect, if he'll come, or at least send someone. Ring the Diocesan Architect's office. Posters. Nice big bright posters, to be lettered by Miss Bellingham's friend who was an artist, summoning Laddenham residents to a Public Meeting to launch the Save our Church Appeal, for display in the public library, at the bus stop, in the newsagent's window, outside the vicarage . . .

*　　*　　*

The primary school playground was full, it being the mid-morning break, as the aeroplanes swept across the sky, and the whole place broke into cheers and an exciting rushing about. Thereafter, for a while, groups of small boys zoomed around in formation until the interest subsided, the impression left by the incident faded, and anyway the bell went and everyone beat it for the school entrance and another hour of enlightened instruction.

*　　*　　*

Martin Bryan, coming home, couldn't remember what day it was. He stopped dead, outside the butcher's (the one with the sign he liked: Meat to Please You, Pleased to Meet You) and didn't know if it was Tuesday or Thursday or what. His head whirled. You needed to know things like that, it was like knowing who you were yourself: Martin Keith Bryan, aged ten, 3 The Green, Laddenham, nr. Spelbury, Oxfordshire, England, Europe, The World, the Universe. And knowing how many people you knew – their names and what they looked like, which was sixty-five he thought, not counting everyone at school which would have brought it up to two hundred and twelve.

What had it been yesterday? It had been a school day, so not a Saturday or Sunday. And the day before had been school but the day before . . . the day before *was* Sunday, so now was Wednesday.

Once more placed in time, he was able to start walking again. He wondered if she'd be at home, if she'd have remembered to get anything for tea. There might be beefburgers. Now, he thought, now at this moment, walking along the High Street, past the White Lion, past the corner where there was sometimes that alsatian he didn't like, now he didn't know at all, it was all emptiness ahead, you couldn't know what there was, it was like looking into a fog. But quite soon, just in minutes, as long as it took the hand on his watch to get from there to there, he'd know, it would all be things that had happened, as though the fog turned into colour, as though shape came from blankness, like Dad's expensive camera that he lost in Jersey last year made pictures come swimming onto squares of paper, just like that, in seconds.

He'd been thinking of that on Sunday, when they'd been driving to see Auntie Judy, Mum and Dad arguing because Dad didn't want to go. He'd sat in the back and seen between their shoulders the dashboard clock saying twelve. When we come back, he'd thought, it'll be saying six, or something like that. I'll be sitting here, like I am now, only then I'll know what happened in between, I'll know things I don't know now, things will have happened that haven't happened yet. He stared over the clock out of the windscreen, at the road advancing and then vanishing. It will actually be like that: I shall sit here and it will be six o'clock. The thought amazed him. And later, when it was so, and he remembered, deliberately, he felt a curious wisdom. He felt older, more than six hours older.

*   *   *

Clare Paling, at her kitchen window, saw the child opposite, that wan-looking little boy, come round the corner followed by, at seven and twelve second intervals, her own son and daughter. All three had the disintegrating look of children at the end of a day's school – jerseys and satchels hung precariously about them, Thomas trailed the sleeve of an anorak in the gutter, the Bryan boy's shirt hung out of his belt at the back. Like swimmers nearing shore, they headed blindly for home, eyes down. Clare watched with detachment, peeling vegetables.

She saw behind the palimpsest faces of her children their own previous selves, their infancy, a fleeting succession of Annas and Thomases slipping through her fingers, gone as soon as they had come. She saw the mobile features of babies settle to individuality; she saw the whole evolutionary process of growth, the curled foetus to the erect child; she heard the amazing flood of language – each precarious second heading for now, this June day, this light pouring through leaves to dapple their unknowing heads. Children live in the moment; the rest of us are saddled with the processes of time.

Thomas, at the lych-gate, looks furtively round to see who may be watching (houses, alas, have eyes, which he has forgotten) and climbs upon the churchyard wall. He balances his way along it, teetering once so that Clare's stomach lurches with him. He flaps his outstretched arms; he is fifty feet high; he towers above the Green majestic in daring and in panic. He is there for ever, suspended at seven years old with the warm stone under his feet and the rolling clouds above his head, while his sister stares in disapproval and intended treachery

32

and his mother goes to the door to call out, to jolt him back into the unyielding present, to bring him sliding down, protesting, denying.

'I *wasn't* going to fall off. And anyway you never said . . .'

And the moment has gone; the clouds have rolled on; the warmth is draining from the stone.

'And anyway,' said Anna piously, 'the vicar wouldn't like it. It's his wall.'

Thomas, in triumph, retaliated. 'It is not. It's God's wall. The church belongs to God, not the vicar, doesn't it Mum?'

'Well,' said Clare, 'technically. . . . Never mind. Tea-time. Milk shakes?'

In the early evening the front door bell rang. Clare, reading in the sitting-room, heard Thomas thump down the hall. Voices. Thomas bounced in to say Mrs Coggan was there.

Sue Coggan stood on the step flanked by her daughters. She contrived, interestingly, to look both neat and distraught at the same time. One child appeared tearful, the other excited. It was at once apparent that this was no routine social call. Sue had already burst into explanations. '. . . Ever so sorry to bother you, but I just couldn't think what else to do, and I knew you've got your car, the mini, you can't help noticing being just opposite. I rang the surgery and they said if it's gone that far in best to take her straight to the Casualty at Spelbury, because they'd have the right instruments there, the doctor wouldn't be able to do anything really.' She stared down at the smallest child; exasperation and embarrassment fought with concern. 'Oh dear, what a silly girl! There we were, all ready for the baths, the water run and everything, and then this! I *am* sorry to bother you, but . . .'

Clare said, 'What's she done?'

'She pushed a button up her nose.'

Anna and Thomas had now gathered to stare. Anna said, 'What kind of button?'

'A pearl button actually. One of John's shirt buttons. Honestly, you wouldn't believe it, would you, I thought at

33

first they were having me on, and then she started crying and . . .'

Clare closed the front door. 'Right. We'd better get going. Don't worry. Jerseys on, Anna and Thomas.'

'I don't want to come,' said Thomas.

'It is illegal,' said Clare, 'to leave children under ten alone in a house, as I've told you before, much that you care. So it's one out, all out, I'm afraid. Jerseys.'

Sue Coggan was now launched on another round of apology. 'Oh dear, of course I didn't think . . . I'd forgotten it would mean taking them all. I feel awful dragging you out. Tracy do stop sniffing and don't hang onto my arm like that. I rang Luxicars in Spelbury but they said forty minutes at least and the doctor said better go as quickly as . . .'

'It's all *right*. Not to worry. Let's go.'

In the car, Anna said, 'If she breathed the button in further would it go right down inside her? Down into her tummy? And then would it . . .' Thomas interrupted. 'It would come out in the end when she . . .'

Clare crashed the gears, bawled 'Shut up! Be quiet both of you or I'll belt you when we get back.'

There was a little indrawn hiss of breath at her side. Sue Coggan shifted Tracy from one knee to another, 'And of course we had to come out just as we were, I didn't like to stop and tidy up for too long, Tracy's got filthy socks on, as I say I was just going to start on the baths. Thank goodness I've got my bag, anyway, and a comb and things, we can have a bit of a clean up when we get there.'

'*Socks*?' said Clare. The windpipe of a five year old child – how wide? One doesn't know about these things, one just imagines, as one does everything, constructs a scenario. Like a hollow plant-stem? Bigger? But not very big. How many holes, the button? Which way round? I'm driving too fast. Think. Which direction is the hospital when you get to the roundabout? Left. Left and then short cut through the industrial estate.

34

'It's going to make them ever so late for bed, I'm afraid, and your two, I *am* sorry. John'll have kittens when he gets in, no tea or anything, I left a note of course, explaining, the thing is it's his late night, he goes over to the other branch. Tracy don't fidget, just sit still, it's very kind of Mrs Paling to take us like this. I turned the oven right off, I've got a cottage pie in, I wondered about leaving it on low but you don't know how long they'll take. I had Tracy in Spelbury General, Mandy was the John Radcliffe in Oxford, of course, before we moved.'

'Mmn?' About another two miles. You can't stop outside the Casualty, it's ambulances only. Drop them off, then find somewhere to park.

'*What* a thing to happen. You just never know, do you, what they'll think of? I mean, medicines, one's careful about, the bathroom cabinet's always locked, but a *button* . . . Honestly, I might have guessed, I walked under a ladder in the High Street this morning, not thinking.' A giggle. 'I thought then, Sue my girl you've got something coming to you. Are you superstitious? I'm afraid I am.'

Christ. Petrol. No, it's O.K. That's all we needed.

'Tracy don't kick Mrs Paling's car seat like that. You don't want a smack, do you?'

Clare said, 'I should keep her as quiet as you can. Never mind the car seat.'

'I love minis. Aren't you lucky. It's V registration, isn't it? I always say to John if only . . .'

'Here we are. I'm going straight to the Casualty Entrance. You get out, with Tracy, and go to the desk. I'll bring the rest when I've parked.'

When she came through the doors, a few minutes later, trailing children, there was no sign of Sue Coggan or Tracy. They sat in a row on tubular chairs with canvas seats; Anna and Thomas fought over the single comic among tattered Sunday newspaper colour supplements. The Coggan child sat docile, swinging her legs. There was no one else there except an old man, hunched into a raincoat, breathing noisily. Nurses clattered along corridors with trolleys.

Anna said, 'Will they cut her open to take it out?'

'No. Be quiet. Give Thomas the bit you've finished with.'

Either you lived with spectres, or they simply were not there for you. Either you waited for the coin to be flipped, at any moment, or you were barely aware of the reverse side. There are two worlds: the real world, in which we live, and pretend we don't, and the world in which bed for little girls is always at seven and the cottage pie is forever cooking nicely in the oven.

Somewhere, a child began to scream. Anna said, 'Is that . . .'

'Let's go and have a walk round outside, you've finished the comic. Come on, Mandy. I think I saw a sweet shop just opposite the hospital gates.'

Mandy said, 'Actually we aren't allowed sweets between meals.'

She had got them outside now, was heading for the gate. 'Never mind. Be a devil. We'll have walnut whips all round, and blow the consequences.'

The point being, of course, that for many the real world hardly ever does rear its ugly head, maybe never until the end and not then if it's short and sharp. You can pass through fairly unknowing, an easy ride. Hunger and pain and panic are somewhere else. In books and newspapers. On the telly. In the past, not nowadays. But for people like me they grin away from the other side of the road; there really is a skeleton at the feast. And yet, and yet . . . And yet given all that, knowing what one knows, there are still moments of absolute, of untouchable felicity. Now is that not curious? Is that not impossible? Account for that, please.

'Can I have another?'

'No. You'll be sick. We'd better go back and see how Tracy is.'

A plastic disc, half an inch or thereabouts in diameter, lodged somewhere in a small pink flesh and blood passage, and which surely if mishandled, if pushed or jolted, must slip back and down instead of forwards and out and then . . . but she could still breathe through her mouth, or could she if it got stuck further down?

Sue Coggan was in the reception hall. Tracy, clutching her hand, looked smug.

'All well. Such a clever man, he fished away with a sort of hook and out it came! Tracy was ever such a brave girl, not a squeak. There, you won't do anything so silly as that again, will you! Honestly though, I didn't know which way to look – not until we got into the cubicle with the doctor did I realize I came out with my apron on, my kitchen apron. What he must have thought!'

'He thought, presumably,' said Clare, 'that you'd been understandably worried about your child.'

'Yes, I s'pose so. Anyway, all's well that ends well, and I really am grateful, I don't know what I'd have done without you. Mandy, what've you got all over your mouth?'

'Chocolate. I'm sorry, my fault. I corrupted her. Shall we go back, then, if Tracy's feeling all right?'

Chapter Four

George Radwell, looking round the village hall, thought they could have done worse. On the other hand, they could have done better. About forty to fifty. Out of three thousand or thereabouts. Well, it was what you would expect. He knew nearly all the faces: churchgoers, or local activists, or both. Mr and Mrs Paling, sitting at the end of the second row, were a surprise. Furtively, he observed them: they stood out, seeming taller and somehow in better health than everyone else. Mr Paling was a good-looking chap.

The Diocesan Architect's assistant presented a suitably gloomy picture, and sat down. George himself had spoken twice, first to open the meeting and introduce the Diocesan Architect's assistant, then to outline his own thoughts about the situation and the preliminary proposals of the Parochial Church Council. Miss Bellingham had interrupted, several times, to make corrections or additions of her own. The chairman of the Parish Council, also, had broken in to make some comment about building costs and estimates. George well knew that he lacked presence; that he was the kind of person who, if speaking, gets interrupted, who seems indeed to invite interruption. When he was young, and had first taken services, it had never ceased to surprise him that the congregation suffered these to proceed without interference. He half expected to have a sermon halted from a back pew; for that reason he always avoided looking at people when preaching. If you kept your eyes down, or trained on the roof, there seemed more of a sporting chance that you'd be allowed a clear run. He tried this now, fixing his gaze on the ladder of stacked chairs at the back of the parish hall. It didn't work. Indeed, the chairman of the Parish Council, rambling off on his own tangent, was only silenced eventually by Mr Paling's crisp suggestion of the formation, here and now, of a working committee to take over the whole question of fund-raising.

George thought, I should have said that.

Names were proposed. Miss Bellingham. The chairman of the Parish Council, Harry Taylor. Mr Coggan. Sydney Porter.

Someone – someone rather deferential at the back, who knew, clearly, who Paling was, and what – wondered if Mr Paling could be persuaded to join the committee.

Mr Paling, regretful but still crisp, said that unfortunately his business commitments took him away from Laddenham so much that he feared he would be somewhat of a broken reed on any committee.

There was a silence. People rustled, looked round to check on who was there.

Mrs Paling, startling George into a twitch that almost overturned the glass of water in front of him, said she had time and energy and would be glad to help. Heads turned, not recognizing the voice, interested. George said er, good, well, thank you very much, Mrs er . . .

'Paling.'

'Of course.'

And behold there was a committee.

* * *

Sydney Porter, as secretary of the Parochial Church Council, made a list of the names put forward. Knowing how things usually fell out, he would probably be secretary of this thing as well. And treasurer, because otherwise it would be Miss

Bellingham, and Miss Bellingham couldn't do book-keeping for toffee. He knew them all, except the tall woman from the other side of the Green. Well, they'd have their work cut out.

*   *   *

Peter said, 'Was the dumpy chap in the green anorak the father of the child in the swallowed button saga?'

'Not swallowed. Up her nose. Yes, that's right. He's the local estate agent. E. J. Coggan & Son. He's Son.'

'Ah.'

'You should live in these parts,' said Clare, 'like me. You get to know a lot.'

'You could come over to Brussels, you know, on one of these trips. Fix up the children with mother, or something.'

'Good. I'll bear it in mind.'

'The vicar seemed a bit of a dimwit.'

'Mmn. And he doesn't much go for me, I suspect. Will I be considered to have been pushy, do you think? Proposing myself.'

'On the contrary, you're just what they need. Ginger things up a bit. More to the point, are you going to find it a drag?'

'That remains to be seen. It'll keep me off the streets, anyway. And I probably care more about the sanctity of the building than they do. In a strictly non-religious sense, of course.'

'Well,' he said, amused, 'I'd never have thought it your scene. A church committee. Daniel in the lion's den.'

'It was Daniel, you may recall, who had the last word.'

*   *   *

George Radwell supposed he would have to be chairman of this fund-raising committee. It would look a bit odd if he weren't. The prospect depressed him, not least because already, in the mind's eye, there loomed the abrasive presence of Mrs Paling and how he would cope with that he did not know. He could see her already, sitting there with that toothy smile and those little pointed breasts, asking awkward questions and saying things that threw you off key so that you said things back that made you appear foolish and you could see yourself as she saw you: foolish. She was a clever woman, no doubt, for what that was worth. Well, if she had some bright ideas about fund-raising maybe it would turn out to be worth having her. But.

But one could have managed very well without. He sighed.

And now there was someone coming up the front path towards the front door. A someone he didn't recognize: a large heavy, middle-aged woman. Mothers' Union business, no doubt, or the preliminaries about a daughter's wedding – could be anything. He went to the door.

She sat on the leather sofa in the study, a massive figure in blue crimplene, hefty knees a little apart so that he had to keep his eyes averted from the shadowy hinterland between and beyond. She had a doughy, expressionless face. At first he could not make head or tail of why she had come. She dumped herself there and seemed to expect him to find out the reason. She was called Mrs Tanner. She lived on the council estate on the far side of Laddenham. She came to church, now and then, Christmas and that. She did not look, on the face of it, like a person in search of spiritual guidance, but then you never knew. George shifted uncomfortably in his chair, fumbling for further conversational openings. And then at last she said it was about her illness.

'Illness?' George eyed her with apprehension. Cancer? Some awful diagnosis? He hoped not; comforting the dying was a thing he never could cope with, his eyes slid from their gaze and his voice loudened with heartiness. She certainly didn't look ill, at all.

'That's why my daughter brought me,' said Mrs Tanner. 'Her that was at the gate, with the little boy. It's this phobia, see. It's been ten years now – ten years this spring. The doctors haven't ever been able to do anything, so my husband said the other day, why not try the vicar? See what he's got to suggest,

41

if anything. Can't do any harm, can it, he said, and that's what they're there for, that sort of thing.'

'Yes,' murmured George, doubtfully, 'yes, quite.' Mrs Tanner stared at him, expectant. She moved a thigh like a bolster and the broken spring in the sofa groaned. George cleared his throat. 'What sort of phobia, Mrs Tanner?'

'That's just it, they can't exactly put a name to it. It's interesting, they say, but it's not quite the straightforward ones. Agoraphobia – that's when you can't go out of doors at all, see.'

'And you don't mind going out?'

'Of course I do,' said Mrs Tanner reprovingly. 'I told you my daughter had to bring me here today, didn't I? I can't go out alone. Nor cross the street nor go in a cinema or a big shop – crowds, see. Nor car journeys.'

'Buses and trains?'

'Not trains. A bus at a pinch, if it's not crowded, so long as my husband's with me, or my daughter.'

George let this sink in for a moment. He asked, 'Then you can't really take a holiday?'

'Well, I wouldn't want to anyway, would I? Not with the way I am about the sea.'

'The sea?'

'I can't look at the sea even in pictures,' said Mrs Tanner impressively. 'Not a calendar or on the telly. If it comes on the telly my husband has to switch off for me.' She stared across at him, her feet planted squarely on the worn vicarage rug, her massive thighs denting the sofa.

'It must cause a lot of difficulties.'

'Difficulties!' Mrs Tanner snorted.

'Could you tell me,' said George delicately, 'what it is you feel – I mean, why it is you don't like to go out alone, or be in a crowd, or go in a car, and so on.'

'Going out alone is animals, in the first place. Dogs. But cats, too. See a dog and I'm a jelly. That's why my husband's always got to be there, in case there's a dog – get between me

42

and it, see. Or my daughter. She comes for me every day and walks me to the shops. Oh, it's no good telling me they don't go for you in the normal way, dogs, I know that. But they *can*. It's been known. For someone with my condition that's all that matters.' She shot a look of triumph at George. 'Then crowds is there might be a fire and you'd not get out. Crossing the street and cars is road accidents.'

'I see,' said George. They sat in silence. Mrs Tanner sniffed, succulently. George went on, with caution 'I suppose one could say – well, all those things are the same for everyone. For all of us. I mean, the chances. It's – well, just the risk of being alive at all.' He gave a little laugh.

Mrs Tanner looked at him with contempt. 'Oh yes. Oh yes, that's been said before. But it's only someone with my condition that *feels* it.'

George said thoughtfully, 'The sea?'

'Heaving like that. What it'ud be like if you were in it.'

George nodded. He couldn't really think of anything much to say. Mrs Tanner gazed fixedly at him. 'They've been seeing me at the clinic seven years now. The old doctor I used to see passed on last March, there's a woman now. Reams of notes they've taken, there's a file that thick.' She measured off an inch or so between finger and thumb; George registered respect. 'They give me drugs and that. I'm on three different ones. They don't make any difference,' she ended complacently.

George began to talk. He talked about stress and pressures and relaxing and seeing things in perspective. He said everyone has their quirks. He said, with another laugh, now with me it's heights, even a stepladder, an ordinary stepladder . . . Mrs Tanner looked across at him, stonily. He rambled on in some desperation and eventually ran dry. Mrs Tanner gathered up her shopping bag and fastened her coat. She said, 'I thought, well, no harm in asking. I said that last night, to my husband, no harm in seeing if there's anything he can suggest.' She moved out into the hall. George opened the door for her; at the gate, a harassed-looking woman with a baby in a pushchair was hanging about. 'My daughter,' said Mrs Tanner. 'She's waiting to see me home. Thank you, Vicar.' She moved away down the path, with a curiously smooth gait, as though she were on castors.

George went back into the study. He felt both unnerved and irritated. The sofa bore, still, the impression of her massive bottom and there was a faint whiff of peppermint. Her jaw, at the points when she had sat in stolid silence, had champed at something. He opened the window and sat down at the desk, where the Restoration Appeal notices awaited him.

*   *   *

Clare, walking the thirty yards from her own door to the vicarage, thought, I wonder who'll be chairman. Not me, anyway, that's for sure. Oh dear, last arrival, there they are all round the table already, that'll be a black mark to begin with. She saw George Radwell get up from his chair, and stood waiting at the vicarage front door, which was badly in need of a coat of paint.

They inspected her, covertly, as George, getting things off to an inept beginning, bumbled through what had to be done and what people had suggested and what he himself was about to propose.

Miss Bellingham thought, those blue canvas trousers like children wear, for a committee meeting, you'd have thought a skirt at the very least, and the jersey's seen better days. John Coggan, receiving across the table Clare's large grin, smiled weakly back and became absorbed in the notepad in front of him; Church Restoration Appeal Comm. he wrote busily, and then the date, twice, and a list of committee members. He would end up as chairman, he supposed: no bad thing, look good in the local papers – Chairman, J. Coggan, Esq. Make a better job of it than the vicar, too. He stretched a leg out, under the table, clipped what must be Mrs Paling's shin, and felt a warm glow creep above his collar; there was something about that sort of woman that made you put yourself in the worst possible light. Harry Taylor, solicitor and chairman of the Parish Council, took his pipe from his mouth and nodded: pity Paling hadn't joined the committee himself, would have been a good idea to get to know him better, one of the high-ups at United Electronics. Sending his wife instead rather put local affairs in their place, not altogether tactful; odd-looking woman, too.

Sydney Porter, taking the minutes, recorded Clare Paling's presence and left it at that.

George Radwell, plunging on, not looking her way, could feel her on his right like the threat of some unstable substance, a fuse that might be sparked off by any unwary movement. He talked faster and worse to cover his unease; incoherence compounded with repetition. Was checked at last by Taylor, wondering smoothly if perhaps the election of some officers, and an agenda, might be an idea at this stage.

John Coggan was elected chairman, Harry Taylor having declined to stand, on the grounds of existing commitments. John Coggan said, 'Well, of course, if that's what the general feeling is, glad to do it. Sure that's all right with you, Vicar?' George, simultaneously offended and relieved, said, too lengthily, that he didn't at all, good heavens no, much better that someone else take over.

They discussed fund-raising methods: sponsored walks and fêtes and raffles and jumble sales.

Harry Taylor said, 'Small beer.'

Miss Bellingham, inferring criticism of a lifetime thus engaged, said huffily that well if Mr Taylor was used to doing things on a bigger scale, Oxfam and all that, then it would be nice if he could give them some ideas. Personally she'd always found that a good summer fête, if the weather was kind . . .

John Coggan remarked that even nowadays fifty thousand was a lot of money.

'What is the church worth,' said Clare, 'on the open market? As a piece of real estate. Just out of interest. Mr Coggan, you know about that kind of thing?'

There was a startled silence. Miss Bellingham pursed her lips and sniffed. George murmured, 'Yes, interesting. I wonder,' and avoided her indignant stare. Next time he was going to make a point of not sitting next to Mrs Paling, not that he'd chosen to this time, she'd just put herself there; out of the corner of his eye, like it or not, he could see her long trousered flanks disappearing under the vicarage dining-room table.

'Well,' said John Coggan, clearing his throat, 'since you ask, I'd be hard put to it to suggest a figure. Not a thing that's ever come my way.' He laughed, a touch embarrassed. 'We had a Methodist chapel once, very bad state of repair. But something like St Peter's . . .' He shook his head.

Miss Bellingham observed that in Norfolk there were churches quite derelict and run down, not used at all, and it was a crying shame. She also thought it was neither here nor there, there were things you couldn't put a price on. Shooting a look at Mrs Paling; a moneyed young woman, you could tell, never mind the clothes, and there was always something just a mite vulgar about moneyed people.

Harry Taylor stoked his pipe and enquired (jovially) if Mrs Paling was suggesting they sell off the chancel.

'It wasn't entirely a frivolous thought,' said Clare. 'It struck me that since we can't possibly rely on churchgoers to give us enough to meet the Appeal, as I'm sure Mr Radwell would agree, in this day and age . . .'

George broke in to agree fervently, and for too long.

'. . . then in that case we have to strike a chord generally. We've got to think of what it is the church has got that most people might feel they wanted to do something for. And what the church has got is age. It's a very old building. And old buildings are well-regarded just at the moment. They have a scarcity value. You know that, Mr Coggan, well enough; antiquity has its price.'

John Coggan agreed that there was always a market for a period house.

'Exactly. So I wasn't meaning that we sell the church. Just that we cash in on its greatest asset. Use it.'

'It's a historical monument,' said Miss Bellingham. 'It says so somewhere. Grade I. Of course some of us,' she went on, not looking at Mrs Paling, 'would feel that that comes second. But still.'

'All churches, virtually' said Clare, 'are of some interest. This one rather more than most. The wall-painting alone . . .'

'It's the Day of Judgement,' instructed Miss Bellingham. 'You've got the saved going up to heaven on one side and the – the unsaved – going down to hell on the other.'

'The damned,' said Clare. 'Quite.' She lit a cigarette.

There was a silence, during which Miss Bellingham could be felt to retract, glower, and gather herself. Sydney Porter, hitherto silent, spoke. He said that he didn't know a lot about that kind of thing, but he'd been looking up one or two books in the library, because he'd been thinking a bit along the same lines as Mrs Paling, since you had to be realistic, and church attendance wasn't that high these days, and it seemed that the church had had quite a bit of history.

'Well, it would, wouldn't it?' snapped Miss Bellingham. 'All that time.'

Harry Taylor came in to say that he thought Mr Porter had a point there, quite a point. There might indeed be something that could be done by way of using the church's historical associations. They had to bear in mind the size of the tourist industry nowadays and while admittedly Laddenham wasn't exactly on the Stratford run it might well be that they could put on something that would pull in a few visitors. We mustn't underrate history.

Miss Bellingham moved in. 'I think that's a very nice idea, Mr Taylor. Very nice. It's what I was just about to suggest myself. A masque, that kind of thing – costume and Good Queen Bess and the schoolchildren could do some maypole dancing. People are very keen on that. I saw the most delightful son et lumière last year at – dear me, I forget exactly, it was a

47

country house somewhere, a very historical place – with lovely music and the actors having a medieval banquet and then dancing and so on, all in costume.'

'That's not history,' said Clare. 'History is ghastly. Nothing but misery and war and brutality. One should be glad it's over.'

Miss Bellingham glanced at her with scorn. What an ignorant and silly remark. It showed Mrs Paling up. She herself thought highly of history and always took some out of the public library on Fridays, along with travel and a couple of thrillers: good biography, like Lady Longford on Queen Victoria, or something on the Greeks and Romans, or a book about stately homes, with nice pictures.

Sydney Porter was speaking again. He said it wasn't history in general that he'd had in mind. It was things particularly to do with the church, with St Peter's, and as far as he could make out from this book he'd found, a book on local history it was, there'd been two quite important things happen actually in the church. At least the first wasn't in the church, it was in the churchyard. There'd been three men shot there.

'Gracious!' interrupted Miss Bellingham. 'Well I don't think that's something we want to be reminded of, do we?'

Shot during the Civil War, in the time of Cromwell and King Charles. These men had been shot by the parliamentary people because though they were on their side, as it were, they weren't toeing the line. They'd got out of hand. Levellers, they called themselves. Lined up against the churchyard wall and shot.

Harry Taylor was attending to his pipe. 'Rough justice!' He looked round the committee, with a little laugh.

George wanted to say something witty that would catch Mrs Paling's attention: something about 'other times, other customs', but that ought to be in French and he didn't know how you pronounced it. He opened his mouth once or twice and shut it again. Finally he came out with, 'Hope it wasn't on a Sunday, at least.'

None of them paid him any attention. Sydney Porter began again.

And then later, in the last century, there'd been a business with a lot of farm workers who'd been demanding higher wages ('Ah!' Harry Taylor interjected, 'now we're getting nearer home. Plus ca change, eh?'). Riots. There'd been threatening letters to landowners and big farmers, just signed 'Captain Swing', about what would be done if they didn't give more money – violence and so on – and the rioters had come to the church and met the parson there, and the local squire, and they'd broken down the altar railings, and messed the place up. In the end, twenty men had been sentenced and transported to Australia.

Miss Bellingham said, 'A lot of them are descended from convicts, out there. Of course they don't like it if it's pointed out too much. My cousin married a person who lives in Sydney.'

Sydney Porter, delivered of his information, was making some notes; meticulous writing, the margin aligned as on the printed page.

Clare lit another cigarette. 'I think that's all very interesting. I think we should find out more about it and see if we can't make some use of it for the Appeal.'

'It's depressing,' said Miss Bellingham.

'History often is.'

John Coggan cleared his throat. That was the trouble with this sort of set-up, broad-based, all kinds of people: you got scrapping. Have to pull things together. He began to summarize the achievement of the evening, insofar as the word was appropriate. The target; the time-scale; the methods. 'And we're all agreed, aren't we, that we should give some thought to making use of the church's history. Some kind of event, perhaps that we could build up to . . .'

'A fête,' said Miss Bellingham, 'with maypole dancing.'

'. . . and hope to draw a wider audience. Perhaps some sort of – well, re-enactment of these incidents Sydney's told us about.'

'Is shooting people an incident?' murmured Clare. 'But I agree that it would be . . .'

Miss Bellingham interrupted to say that she didn't see how you re-enacted that, not authentically.

John Coggan ignored her. And with this in view, he went on, perhaps Sydney and er, Mrs Paling maybe since she was enthusiastic about the idea, could put their heads together and find out some more about the background and what actually happened and so forth and then the committee could talk about it again at the next meeting.

The committee dispersed. Clare, looking back for a moment as she went out of the vicarage gate, saw George Radwell at the uncurtained window, staring out and then turning away hastily as he caught her eye. There's a bloke who doesn't care for me one little bit, she thought, oh well, it's mutual, come to that. And now for bed and a good book, after that lot. Or a good husband.

And as she turned into her own driveway the motorbike boys roared past, an explosion of noise and wake of acrid smell, reminding her of those aeroplanes. One, two, three, four, five, six – crouched figures, carapaced and goggle-eyed – tearing round the Green, and then round again, peeling off finally down the High Street and away.

Chapter Five

George, going through to the kitchen to make himself a cheese sandwich before bed, heard the bike boys and was reminded, disagreeably, of his time in Stoke Newington, which he would have preferred to forget. The Youth Club and the Church Hall disco and the milling derisive young with whom he could not cope. And the breezy confident vicar and his acolytes, those long-haired quick-talking women in trousers and hairy sweaters, who bore, he now realized, a distant relationship to Mrs Paling.

He ate the sandwich, and then went up. He undressed, washed, got into bed, switched the light out and lay for a while with his eyes open.

He proceeded with the business of making love to Mrs Paling. First he put her on the vicarage sofa, stripped to a pair of peach-coloured knickers, and dwelt for a while on the removal of these. But, arousing as this was, the satisfaction of the arrangement was marred by the twang of the spring in the sofa. Irritated at this insistent accuracy of the imagination, George removed Mrs Paling to a sunny woodland glade, all birdsong and vibrant nature. Here, for a while, things went nicely: the lady moaned and spread; George performed with skill and consideration; bodies writhed and twined, dappled by sunlight. And then Clare Paling turned her horsy, handsome, supercilious face towards him and laughed in mockery and contempt.

Shrivelled with self-disgust, George sat up in bed, put the light on, and reached for Ngaio Marsh.

The telephone, next morning, brought him from his breakfast, mouth still full of toast. A coin-box call, pips going for an age, then a woman's voice he knew but couldn't place. 'That the vicar?' 'Yes?' 'It's Mrs Tanner.' Tanner? The phobia woman; his heart sank. 'It's about you not having anyone to come in, my daughter heard at the doctor's. I don't mind giving it a try, see how we get on. I been talking it over with my husband and we both think it might get me out of myself a bit. There's no animals, is there?' He played for time: 'What?' 'Two mornings a week, she was doing, Shirley Binns, that right?' 'That's right,' he said weakly. 'But are you sure you really . . .' 'Monday I'll start then, Vicar. As I say I'll give it a try. My daughter'll walk me there and pick me up later.' The phone clicked.

He went back to the kitchen, and looked round. It was infested with crumbs and spattered with grease, had been since Shirley went off to have her baby. He would have cleaned it up eventually, just as he'd had a go with the carpet-sweeper in the dining-room before last night's committee. He didn't want that awful woman here, two days a week; he groaned; no way of stopping her now, he didn't even know how to get hold of her. In gloom, he walked across to the church.

There was a movement somewhere beyond the gravestones at the far end of the churchyard, he thought, squinting into the sun from the gate. Better investigate; there'd been trouble a few months back with children playing there and interfering with flowers on the tended graves. But then the striking clock reminded him how late it was and he went into the porch.

* * *

If you lay on your stomach in the long grass behind the stones no one could know you were there; you could fire at them as they came through that gate, bang-bang, and you'd got them before they had a chance. Bang-bang. Bang you're dead.

There were dead people under the ground here. Under where he lay, maybe. Skeletons. He wondered how far down they were. Did the bones ever stick up above the graves? All the stones had writing on them; often you could read it: Elizabeth Frances Hicks, born April 16th 1871, died October 7th 1942. Departed this life. Rest in peace. Martin Paul Bryan, born May 10th 1970.

He didn't want to go to school today. He felt funny inside. He'd stay here for a bit, go later, say he'd been sick and his mother'd let him stay at home.

He rolled onto his back and stared at the sky, ground his knuckles into his eyes to make coloured patterns shower across his lids, tried to forget the feeling in his stomach, tried to forget last night.

He'd heard their voices downstairs in unpretending anger; open, intense and intimate anger, like people in films or on the telly. In real life people do not talk to each other like that. He lay stiff under the bedclothes, listening; for a while, in hope, he had thought perhaps it *was* the telly. And then the hope had crumbled and left him with his stomach drained, empty as though he was hungry, but sick too. And down below that noise; all feeling and no words, not words you could hear. It was as though something strange and full of evil had crept into the house: an animal, a dark furtive animal, padding around the stairs and hall, with rank fetid breath. Nowhere was safe, not even his home. In the end, he hugged his pillow to his ears, and slept.

* * *

George found the church door was unlocked; Sydney Porter must have been in already for some reason. As churchwarden, he held the spare set of keys. There had been a time, last year, after the disappearance of a brass cross from the Lady Chapel and an attempt to break open the offertory box, when they had considered keeping the church permanently locked. George, anticipating the nuisance of continual callers at the vicarage wanting it opened, had been as reluctant as anyone to do this. In the end, they had compromised by locking up earlier in the evenings, with George and the churchwardens alternating a duty rota of policing visits during the daytime. So far, there had been no further trouble.

There was a starling in the vestry, trapped, thumping against the window. Droppings littered the table; it must have been there all night. George opened the door and saw it fly down the nave and come to rest on one of the capitals, where it shuffled along the head of a foliate mask, making more mess. He went back to the vestry to fetch a broom. When he returned Sydney Porter was already brandishing a pole at the bird, which flew up to one of the windows. Sydney said, 'There's been those children in the churchyard again. Grass is all flattened at the back of the hedge.'

'Ah. Have to keep an eye out.'

They stood looking at the starling, fluttering against the stained glass, which depicted a ripple-bearded Noah in a storm-tossed medieval ship. 'We won't get it down,' said Sydney. 'Best thing's just to leave the door open for the morning.'

George nodded. 'Quite a good meeting last night. Got things off the ground.'

'That's right.'

'Tactful move, I felt, to hand over the chairmanship to Mr Coggan. We want to get the village involved as a whole.'

Sydney continued to watch the starling, non-committal.

'Mrs Paling,' George went on, after a pause, 'could turn out to be a bit of a live wire, I should imagine.' He, too, studied the Noah window. 'She and I were having a chat about the church the other day, the Doom painting and so forth – knowledgeable sort of woman. Good-looking, too.'

The vicar, Sydney now noticed with surprise, was agitated; a nerve twitched in his cheek, his complexion was blotchy. He wondered what was up. The conversation was taking an odd turn, too, these remarks about Mrs Paling. Exchanges between them, normally, were confined entirely to matters of expediency: keys and hymnals and weddings and organ music and the flower-arranging rota. Well, it was nothing to do with him, nothing to get involved with.

'Calls herself an agnostic,' said George Radwell. 'Not that that bothers me at all – it takes all sorts, as far as I'm concerned. No, no – that doesn't worry one. Question of personal choice, and that's all there is to it.'

Sydney shuffled in discomfort. He didn't like that sort of talk, least of all from the vicar. It was embarrassing. He looked around for a way of escape.

'I said to her, look, Mrs Paling, I'm as broad-minded as the next man, your beliefs are your own concern, and whatever they are you and your family are very welcome in the parish, glad to have you with us.'

The starling flew across the nave, crashed into the War Memorial window on the west wall and thumped to the ground.

'Ah,' said Sydney gratefully, 'pity. They're always doing that. I'll put it in the incinerator.'

He left George standing there, and carried the bird outside into the churchyard. But there, holding it in one hand, he saw the tremor of movement in one grey eyelid and felt, he fancied, a shiver in the light body. It must be stunned, not dead. He set it down gently on the grass and watched it. The bird lay motionless and now he knew what it was that had been itching away in his mind while the vicar had been talking, like a message forgotten, like an obligation over-looked.

Jennifer had found a dead bird once, in the Mansell Road garden, what passed for a garden, the scrubby London back yard. Jennifer when she was eight, a thin child with plaits wearing a green and white checked cotton frock, standing at the kitchen door with the bird in her hands. And he had gone into the garden with her and dug a hole in the sour ground and buried it with her looking on, solemn. She had wanted him to put a cross with sticks, and he had explained that wasn't right,

55

not for a creature, that was only for people. Late in 1940 that would have been, his last leave with them, the last time he saw them.

Except the very last time, in the mortuary. He'd asked to go, though there was no need, the identifying had been done already, before he came up from Portsmouth, done by the A.R.P. Warden, who was a neighbour, who knew them well. They were side by side, and the attendant had pulled back the sheet that covered Mary first and for a moment he'd been shattered anew, thought wildly that perhaps there could have been a mistake, because her hair was grey, quite grey, her short, fine, brown hair. And then he'd realized it was the plaster, the plaster dust that had spewed out of the house as it fell about them, covering them, drowning them, suffocating them. And he had stood there staring not at her face, which was grey-white too, but at her dusty hair, until at last someone put a hand on his arm and steered him away.

Perhaps the starling would revive; if not, he would deal with it later. He didn't like to see the churchyard untidy, from time to time he went through the long grass by the wall with a plastic bag in his hand, stuffing into it the rubbish that found its way from the pub car park.

*   *   *

Mr Porter from next door came out of the church holding something, which he put down on the grass by the path. Then he stood there, for ages, for hours, it seemed, staring at the ground. When at last he went away Martin had pins and needles from keeping still, crouched down behind the big stone chest thing (those had dead people in, too) under the yew tree. Mr Porter had nearly seen him before, when he'd walked over to the wall, and Martin had had to slither off quickly, keeping low.

He slipped out, cautiously. It was a bird, a dead bird. But no, not dead, because as he approached it lurched suddenly onto stick-like legs and stood swaying and blinking. It must be hurt,

56

poor thing. He was filled suddenly with a surge of warm pro-
tective feeling: he would look after it until it was better, he
would take it home and feed it and it would be his bird, it would
be tame, it would come when he whistled. He picked it up.

*　　*　　*

Clare, circling the Green on her way back from the school,
stopped the car and wound down the window. 'Morning, Mr
Porter.' Oh God, now she'd made the poor man jump out of
his skin.

'Good morning, er . . .'

'We'd better put our heads together at some point.'

'Heads . . .?'

'This stuff we're going to do on the history of the church –
the civil war thing and the other.'

'Oh. Oh, yes.'

'Where did you find out about it – what book?'

'There's that booklet in the library, the village library –
History of Spelbury. It mentions Laddenham and the other
villages.'

'Would it be an idea,' said Clare, 'if I went further afield, to
one of the bigger county libraries, to see if I could lay hands on
a few more books, and then we can go through them together
and see what we can come up with?'

'Fair enough.'

Not the most forthcoming person in the world. Or is it just
my genius for alienation?

'If you've the time,' he added.

That's better; we'll win him over yet. Big smile. 'Oh, I've
plenty of time, Mr Porter. Well, I'll be seeing you, then.'

All the time in the world. And for a book-junkie like me a
trip to the county library is right in the line of business. In fact,
come to think of it, there's no time like the present. Quick
sprint home to make the beds and then off. Not a bad prospect
at all, the day looks more promising already. So wave nicely to
the vicar since we're feeling genial, and away.

The days are not unpromising, it's not that; Peter is wrong in his diagnosis of bored housewife. Peter, of course, has been trained to spot problems and then apply his considerable talents to solving them. Which is all very well where assembly lines and productivity targets and technical innovations are concerned but not always so effective when it comes to people. No, I am not bored.

Children are bored, because they live in a continuous present and want to escape. The old are bored, for other reasons. When I was a child I never believed I would grow up. Now I am grown I watch my own survival with disbelief. And the survival of those I love. I can look at a fourteenth century wall painting of Judgement Day with the understanding and apprehension of a fourteenth century peasant. Unlike the twentieth century priest next door, who is in other respects more ignorant and less worldly than I take myself to be. So much for sophistication.

It's a crude threat, that division into the damned and the saved; as crude as the weighing of souls. All to induce guilt – guilt and therefore compliance. Do as I say, or else. Nowadays we are less gullible, but we still feel guilt: different guilts. When I contemplate the day of judgement it is not the possibility of salvation I have in mind.

When I was a child I tried to be good – to begin with because people were pleased if you were good and later because I had developed theories about the nature of goodness. I thought it was wrong to be cruel to animals or those weaker than yourself; I reckoned you should be polite, up to a point; I tried to treat others as I should like them to treat me, though I suspected a flaw somewhere in that argument. Later, I went through the Ten Commandments; most of them were straightforward enough, but some didn't seem to apply to me and there was a hectoring note that I found distasteful. And later still my unbelief blossomed and I ceased to accompany my parents to church on Sundays and my mother was upset. I explained to her that I probably shared her every opinion on what was right and what was wrong, but I could not believe in God. I said I believed in love and she said God is love and I said, no. And after that we avoided the subject.

No, my days are not empty; in fact, I find them miraculous. The legacy, I think, of telling people for a thousand years that they will have to pay for their sins is that you end up with someone like me. I wait for payment to be exacted anyway. I feel guilty because it has not.

She made the beds, went downstairs and out again. Back in the mini, she sped between fleeing fields, hills, villages. Driving too fast, reproved once by an overtaking lorry, the driver in his cab towering above her, cutting in front and forcing her to slow down. Peter scolded her sometimes about her driving. Once he'd been really angry after a near accident. Tempting providence, he called it. Providence doesn't need tempting, she'd snapped, that's the problem, as far as I'm concerned. But the incident had rattled her (accounting for the ill temper), as now she was rattled by the thunderous pressure of the lorry alongside. She drove more decorously, paying attention to the charms of the landscape.

I love my husband, she thought. I look around at other people's husbands, at other men generally, and heave a sigh of relief. His deficiencies, if one can call them that, are that he is too busy and too successful and I am no longer the only or indeed the principal person with a claim on him. I love my husband and therefore I will try to do as he would wish and not drive too fast.

There were huge clouds piled around the horizon, the cumulus clouds of early summer, opalescent shifting shapes, themselves a source of light so that the whole sky was brilliant. On such a day as this, she remembered, on such a day of sun and shadow and high running wind, she had climbed a hill somewhere, almost ten years ago, and at the top had flung herself down breathless on her back and stared up into just such clouds and as she did so had felt the first flutter of the child in her womb. A moment of amazement and delight and incredulity. Thus are the heightened moments of our lives tethered to the physical world, and brought back by it. Well, that interesting flutter was now Anna – screaming and whooping in Laddenham primary school playground – but the joyous instant on the hilltop one carried around yet, as something else.

The town, with which she was not familiar, although it was only fifteen miles from Spelbury, had a stern attitude towards on-street parking and the municipal car parks were all full. Eventually she found a space in the far corner of a cindery, rubbish-strewn overflow car park, tucked away the mini and set off for the public library.

The library, plate glass without and sleekly carpeted within, was a new building. The shelves were well-stocked, the catalogue abundant, the squashy black chairs and individual desks invited repose or study. Clare, well pleased, browsed and dipped and selected for an hour or so. In the Local History section, an agreeable and obliging young man answered her queries and provided references and information. Waiting for him to bring some books, she noted with approval that the reading desks were almost all occupied by teenagers, in refuge perhaps from inadequate school facilities, heads bowed tranquilly over their work.

Going into the ladies' lavatory on the way out, she found herself in a cubicle the walls of which were covered with graffiti of startling sexual crudity. Long masturbatory fantasies involving carrots or sausages were interspersed with drawings of male and female genitals, separately and in conjunction, and clinical accounts of the writers' own sexual exploits. Clare sat reading, in interest and amazement. One could fancy oneself in the latrines of some army barracks, not the ladies' lavatory of the public library in a midland market town. The handwriting, in tempo pen, biro and occasionally aerosol paint, was almost exclusively the unformed script of, it seemed to her, children. Or adolescents at the most. She thought again, a little perturbed, of the docile studious figures at the desks overhead.

Surely not? She came out, washed her hands, gathered up her armful of books, and set off once more for the car park.

Heading for the corner in which she had left the car she could not at first see it. Where it had been – where she thought it had been – was a red Ford Capri. Then, as she got nearer, she saw that the Capri had been parked in front of the mini, boxing it in. The mini was at the end of a line of cars, up against a wall; the Capri sat blandly eighteen inches ahead of its front bumper.

She tried the door handles. Locked, of course. Similarly the legitimately parked car alongside the mini; no possibility of a manoeuvre there. Fuming, she noted the car park ticket pasted to the Capri's windscreen: three hours yet to run.

She sat in the mini for fifteen minutes. Then, for a further thirty, searched the car park, surrounding streets and adjacent car park for a traffic warden or attendant. None to be seen. Nor yet a policeman.

She returned to the car. Sat, another fifteen minutes. Paced the car park, another fifteen. Received the commiserations of the driver of a departing Morris, three cars down the line. Contemplated an act of aggression against the Capri, made a note of its number (which one was not going lightly to forget, in any case). Smoked a fifth cigarette. Read three pages of a book. Sat. Paced. Sat.

A man and a woman approached. He, suede jacketed, with droopy moustache, side-burns, round shouldered, early thirties. She, tight-legged white canvas trousers, high-heeled boots, strawberry blonde hairdo glinting with lacquer, pushing forty. The man had his key in the Capri's door as Clare rose from the mini.

'Just a minute.'

'Eh?'

'I have been sitting here now for an hour and a half.'

A silence. The woman, patting her hair, embarrassed. The man, car door open now, throwing a pile of order books into the back, 'Well, then?'

Monumental stupidity may of course be indistinguishable

61

from massive indifference to the convenience of others. 'Because,' said Clare, 'you parked your car in such a way as to make it impossbile for me to get out.'

He took his jacket off, hung it with care on a hook fixed to the interior of the car, began to get in.

'Oh no,' she said, loudly now, some passers-by turning to stare, 'oh no. This won't do. What about it?'

'What about what?'

'The fact that you have considerably inconvenienced me.'

He straightened, looked at her. The woman said, 'Let's go, Keith!'

'It happens,' he said. 'It's one of those things, I'm afraid. Could happen to anyone.'

A few people were hovering now, interested. Clare closed the door of the mini, slowly, and took a couple of steps forwards. 'Really? You astonish me. Could it, indeed?'

'That's right.'

'It doesn't bother you – disturb you just in the very slightest – that you've made a nuisance of yourself to someone else?'

'Oh look,' the woman began, 'let's forget it. I've got to be . . .'

'I can't say it does, lady,' he said.

Clare stood now immediately beside the right headlamp of the Capri. 'Ah. And are you thinking of making me an apology?' It came to her, with a pleasurably heady sensation that it might be possible to kick in the headlamp.

'No. I can't say I am.'

Damn it to hell, she had sandals on, not her good clumpy shoes.

'You're not?'

He was getting into the car now, had reached across to unlock the door for the woman. 'Ah,' said Clare. She stood over him now, and went on in a conversational tone, but loudly enough to retain the interest of the few bystanders, 'Then listen to me. One comes across some fairly disagreeable outlooks on life but for sheer blatant gall yours just about takes the biscuit. Your wife there must be proud of you. A fine display of sticking to one's principles that was.' He was trying to shut the door. Clare tugged at the handle and went on. 'It would be interesting to see a real three star performance, for private consumption. I take it that was just the economy model, for dealing with stray members of the public. By the way, you've got some of the prawn cocktail you had for lunch on your tie.' She slammed the door at the same moment as the Capri's engine spat into life and the car shot forward.

She got back into the mini. The bystanders were all departing hastily, like people determined not to have witnessed a street accident. Clare, breathing a little heavily, tidied her hair, checked on purse, library books, keys, and drove off.

On the way home she began to laugh. Well, well. I quite enjoyed that. A spell of rage is oddly stimulating. Pity it never came to physical violence. I'm bigger than he was.

Chapter Six

Sydney Porter couldn't think where Tasmania was. It had bothered him last night, when he went to bed, late, much later than his usual time. He had sat reading so long that when he looked out of the front door, before locking up, to see what the weather was doing, all the lights were out round the Green. And then he'd lain awake, bothered about Tasmania.

After breakfast, he went to the book-case and got out the atlas. His school atlas, it had been. Bartholomew's. But not right now, a lot of it, too much pink – all those places belonging to us then, that no longer do.

Tasmania was an intermediate colour: lilac, for Commonwealth. He stared at the double page spread. It would have taken the devil of a long time to get down there, in those days. Months. He should know – the long weeks to Bombay, in 1944, round the Cape, in the old *Reliant*, escorting convoys. Weeks of tedium, broken by the tension of an attack. You came almost to hope for a bit of action, in madder moments. Weeks of heat and discomfort and the cramped mess deck.

He thought of those villagers, those men who'd been convicted after the business in the church. Podd and Lacy and Binns and the rest. Battened down in stinking holds. Seasick and wretched. Knowing they'd never see their homes and families again. Poor devils. And all for talking out of turn, for getting a bit het up, for wanting a fair wage. Well, it wasn't like that now, and a good thing too, not that he'd ever been that much of a socialist himself, but it made you think, reading this kind of thing. Poor sods.

He turned the page, to the Far East, the names making him think now of the war: Singapore and Java and the Philippines. Images came and went in his mind like a series of projector slides: Podd and Lacy and Binns, ragged ineffectual figures with country accents herded into some creaking ship; troops streaming up the gangway of the *Ranchi* at Portsmouth in 1940, hung about with kit, waving three deep from the rails; the dust and debris and broken glass in Mansell Road, Mary's plaster-whitened hair. He saw people hustled hither and thither, blown by terrible mindless winds, helpless, hapless. He saw too, suddenly, the wall-painting in the church and the grey figures bundled away by red devils or stern condescending angels. A Doom painting, the church guide-book said; 'Doom wall-paintings, Day of Judgement scenes, were common in medieval churches and served as a pictorial reminder to the illiterate congregation of the brevity and insecurity of life and the perils of non-repentance.' Forgive us our trespasses. Deliver us from evil. Ha bloody ha, he thought in sudden fury. He was trembling, he realized. Alarmed by his own feelings, he put the atlas back in the book-case and went out into the garden, where he took down the large fork and set about a systematic dig of the plot in which, next week, he would plant out young cabbages.

He had been saved from thought, after the bomb, by the posting to the Med and all that that implied. He hadn't cared, one way or the other, if he died himself. But he hadn't died; he'd survived to go on to the tedium of the Bombay run and eventually to Portsmouth again and being demobbed and finding a job and somewhere to live. There was a padre who had tried to talk to him from time to time, meaning well, had him on a list, no doubt: keep an eye on this man. A nice enough

65

bloke; trouble was, they couldn't think what to say to each other. The padre would bumble on and grind eventually to a halt, and Sydney would nod and then there'd be a silence; both of them, Sydney supposd, not being fools, knew that in the end there was nothing to be said. The padre talked of faith and the comfort of prayer and the love of God; he talked to Sydney as one believer to another. What he didn't know, could never have explained, was that it was order Sydney sought, and found, in the Church, rather than any of that. The order of things said and done each time in the same way, the order of knowing that nothing could interfere with how those things were said and done, the knowledge that this order had gone before and would go on after, that it survived the chaos of everything else.

For the rest of his life all he wanted was order. To move from day to day without disturbance; to know that day would follow day; to anticipate with some accuracy what the next day might hold. He had lost everything. For the rest of his life he would have nothing, so that that might never happen again. No more love; no more commitment. They can't take away from you what you haven't got. He would live on the foothills, expect little and risk little.

He moved away from London in the mid-fifties to the job in Spelbury and bought the Laddenham house. Even that seemed to him rash; he was choosing the place with an eye to retirement. A quiet place with a good garden on light soil.

You took no risks, gardening; your only commitment was to the seasons, which never fail. Small disappointments, yes; minor triumphs. And you could safely plan, knowing that till the end of time, come what may; summer will follow spring, there will be growth and fruition and decay. There is a natural order, if no other. Sydney dug and planted and reaped again. And again. And again.

This year he intended trying a new cabbage: Autumn Giant. He wiped the tines of the fork clean and hung it in its

66

place in the tool-shed. His anger had subsided; he felt himself once more. Now he would do some reading, because Mrs Paling wanted those books back by the end of the week. Reading and making notes, carefully, his memory wasn't what it was and he wouldn't be able to keep tabs on all those facts and dates without. He was no scholar, but he'd work something out, and he didn't want to look silly in front of Mrs Paling when it came to writing up their piece for the committee.

He'd felt obliged to offer her a cup of tea when she brought the books over; she stood there in the hall, grinning away, with no sign of leaving, and in the end he had to ask her to come through and sit down. He hadn't really wanted to get involved, but you couldn't be too un-neighbourly.

She sat drinking her tea with those long thin trousered legs stuck out in front of her. He put the biscuit tin on the table, the Coronation biscuit tin from Mansell Road, and she picked it up and said, goodness, you only ever see those in antique shops nowadays, with some ridiculous price on, nice to see one being used. And then went red and started off about something else and he realized she was embarrassed, thought she'd dropped a brick, making out his things were old-fashioned. And realized too she was quite a nice woman, really, even if a bit off-putting with that sharp way of talking and a strung-up feeling about her, as though she had to hold herself back all the time.

He said, 'I gave it to my wife for her birthday, one year.'

She looked at the biscuit tin again, and then at him; trying to put two and two together, no doubt.

'My wife was killed in an air-raid, second year of the war. And the little girl.'

She couldn't know the compliment that was. He didn't often tell anyone that, only let it leak out when it had to. Particularly not women; there was a kind of woman never let you alone once they knew, women he'd worked with at Robinsons, or neighbours; as though you were a cripple, to be smothered with kindness. Somehow, he didn't think Mrs Paling was that type; dropping in with home-made cakes to see you were getting on all right, sharp eyes looking over your shoulder and into the kitchen, or up the stairs, wondering how you managed, what it felt like.

She went on holding the biscuit tin, staring at the oval-framed faces of the king and queen. She said, 'How appalling,' in a low voice, and then, 'Thirty-nine years ago.'

Sydney said, 'Won't you take a biscuit?'

She took a coffee cream and put it in her saucer. She wasn't going to eat it, you could see; it was done out of politeness.

Mrs Paling began to talk about the books she'd brought. She gave him a piece of paper on which she'd made a note of the chapters and page numbers that had most about what they were looking for. From the way she talked, Sydney guessed she knew a fair bit more about historical things than he did, not that she was trying to patronize or anything, it just slipped out. He nodded and made one or two remarks – cautious, unrevealing remarks. They agreed to meet again when Sydney had had time to do some reading, and draft some sort of report for the committee. Mrs Paling said drily that when Sydney read about the transportations he'd probably agree with her that it wasn't quite the jolly sort of history Miss Bellingham had in mind. But then, she said quietly, I don't imagine you feel history's all that jolly, Mr Porter. Thanks very much for the tea, I'd better dash, the kids'll be back from school and if I'm not there they start pulling the place to pieces. Bye. See you.

Sydney put the biscuit she hadn't eaten back in the tin; waste irritated him. He cleared away the tea things. Then he arranged the books in a pile on the coffee table in the lounge, with slips of paper marking the right places, and set to reading what was to be read.

When he finished he was oddly shaken; involved, as though what he'd been reading was fiction, novels, thrillers – not things in history books, over and done with. You never thought of all that as having to do with you personally. You never thought of yourself as being part of the same process. Now, remembering Mrs Paling's remark, thinking of Podd and Lacy and Binns, he saw suddenly an unending remorseless sequence; people harried and cut down, Christians, Jews, fanatics, prophets, stubborn religious soldiers, disgruntled country labourers, Mary and Jennifer.

* * *

Keith Bryan, standing at the downstairs toilet, jumped violently. There was this cardboard box on the floor, that he hadn't noticed when he went in, and suddenly something started shuffling inside it. He zipped himself up and stooped over the box; there were holes stabbed in the lid with a pencil, and this crawling, shuffling from inside. Martin. Bloody little wretch. Christ alone knew what . . . If there was one thing Keith hated it was rats. He shuddered, and slammed out of the room in search of Shirley. This just about put the lid on it for today; he was still rattled from that business with the woman in the car park, all in front of Debbie Comstock. Not that he hadn't coped with the silly bitch and afterwards he and Debbie had had a laugh about it, maybe in the end it might actually have sent his stock up a bit with Debbie, you never knew. At least he'd let that woman know where she got off.

Shirley was watching the telly. Of course; what else? He said, 'What's in that bloody box in the toilet?'

'It's a bird. Some bird Martin brought in.'

'Well, I didn't think it put itself there, did I?'

She kept her eyes glued to the box: the two Ronnies. He'd watch himself, for two pins, but he was still all het up.

'I said: did I?'

'Eh?'

He reached out and switched the set off. Now he had her attention, for what it was worth. God, what a slag she looked, after Debbie Comstock: trousers that did nothing for her, sweater with stains down the front, frizzy hair that hadn't seen a comb since this morning.

'Do you mind?' she said. 'I was watching that.'

'And I want to know about this bloody bird. What did you let him bring it in for?'

She shrugged. 'Why not? Shut up, Keith, you'll have him down here.'

'I'm putting it out of the back door.'

She shrugged. 'O.K., suit yourself.' She had her hand out towards the telly. He got between her and the set. 'And there's no bloody beer in the fridge. I told you to get some from the supermarket.'

'Fuck you,' she said, angry now. 'That's not all I've got to do, traipse around looking after your wants.'

'And what exactly have you got to do, eh? Eh? You tell me, then. What have you got to do? Sit about on your bum all day, that's what.'

'And what else can I do, stuck here? There's no jobs, is there?'

'Not for someone looking like you do, too right. You want to smarten yourself up a bit, Shirley, I told you that the other day. You look a proper slag these days.'

'Oh, belt up. You're no Steve McQueen yourself, with the pot belly you're getting.'

The door must have opened without him hearing. Martin was standing there. He said uncertainly, 'Dad?'

Shirley said, 'Get off upstairs, Martin, there's a good boy. You can take a jaffa cake from the tin in the kitchen.'

'I didn't know Dad had come in. I wanted to show him my . . .'

The T-shirt he wore was stained down the front just like Shirl's sweater: irritation surged in Keith. The pair of them, what a dump to come back to every evening, no wonder he felt so bloody cooped up, caged in, held back. 'And that bird or whatever it is has got to go, do you hear? If your mum had any sense she'd have said so straight away.'

70

'*Why*? It's not doing any harm. I'm going to make it tame, and train it, and . . .'

'I don't see why he shouldn't keep the bird,' said Shirley. 'Trust you – spoil anything for anyone, you would.'

'If I say it's to go, it's to go.'

'Mum said . . .'

'I don't bloody care what she said. You put it out tomorrow morning, do you hear?'

Martin went out of the room, banging the door.

'Finished?' said Shirley. 'Had enough? Satisfied?'

He felt suddenly weary, done in, fed up, 'Oh, shut up, Shirl.'

She switched the telly on. The room was flooded with laughter. He flung himself down on the sofa, the far end from her. She was smiling now, eyes on the screen. After a minute he began to grin; they were bloody funny, those two, no getting away from it, he'd have to remember that line.

*   *   *

The house was full of laughter. He sat on the edge of his bed and laughter came up through the floor. He shuffled through his pile of comics, looking for one he might not have read for a while. He didn't know how much he minded about the bird, really. It had strange reptilian eyes and he didn't like the cold scaly feel of its clawed feet. It smelt nasty, too. he wished he could have a dog. There wasn't much chance, he knew, that he ever would. Not till he was grown-up.

Downstairs, the laughter. In his stomach, that clenched lump again, hurting. He read a comic, his face contorted into a scowl.

*   *   *

'Why are we going to church?'

'For various reasons.'

'But you don't believe in God.'

71

'Tidy your hair,' said Clare.

'Do you?'

'Shoe laces, Thomas.'

'Do you, Mummy?'

'No.'

'Then why?'

'To have a look,' said Clare briskly. 'That's what. See if it's all going on as I remember. Come on.' She bundled them towards the door. 'There, that's for the collection.'

'Have I been christened?'

'You know perfectly well you haven't.'

'Julie Stevens says if you haven't been christened you go to hell when you die.'

'Julie Stevens is talking rubbish.'

'Where is hell?' Thomas, walking very slowly eighteen inches ahead of one, so that rising irritation is tempered by that melting of the vitals produced by the sight of the back of his neck, of such downy delicacy that one never ceases to marvel, and lament.

'There's no such place. Tom, could you not walk just in front of me.'

'Then why do people talk about it?'

'Because . . . Well, in the old days I suppose because they needed to frighten each other.'

'Why do they now, then?'

'They don't.' Thomas, again, dropping his collection money in the gutter and stooping to retrieve it with that grace, that stylish folding of bony limbs, that makes the movements of children a perpetual delight. One's own miraculous children above all.

'You just have yourself, stupid. So does Julie Stevens.'

'Anna darling, Julie Stevens is not an oracle. I suppose nowadays people think hell isn't a separate place, but a part of things.'

'What things?'

I am all for candour with children, she thought, but this

conversation is getting a bit beyond me. 'Well, just the way things are some of the time. Tom, please don't scuff your shoes like that.'

'There's the Coggans.'

There indeed; father, mother, and little girls in matching pink dresses with spanking white socks.

'I don't believe in God either,' said Thomas, 'or Jesus. Or angels and things. I think it's stupid.'

'You aren't old enough to decide yet. And don't talk so loudly.'

'Why not? Aren't you allowed to say you don't believe in God outside the church?'

'Just shut up, will you?' hissed Clare. 'Be quiet. And once inside, sit still.'

*   *   *

George, in the middle of the Venite, caught sight of Clare Paling, stood transfixed, in silence, for the next two sentences, pulled himself together, and fixed his eyes resolutely on the undisturbing person of Sydney Porter in his accustomed place beside the aisle at the back of the church. She was flanked by her children. What, exactly, was she doing here? And what, if anything, was one to say to her, given that one was almost bound to find oneself within a yard or two in the porch afterwards? Nothing? Some sharp comment? A chat with the children? Now he was off his stride, flustered, would have to contend for the rest of the service with that looming problem and the present problem of how to look at the congregation while not looking at Mrs Paling. How to avoid, above all, catching her eye.

*   *   *

Sue Coggan, rising to her feet, checking quickly on her children (behaving nicely, looking sweet: all well) glanced round the church and saw with surprise Mrs Paling and her two (fidgety, dressed all anyhow: hmn . . .). Well, goodness, she's not a churchgoer, not normally. But of course she's on this committee, I s'pose she felt she should.

Mrs Paling, Sue noted, made no pretence at joining in the hymn but appeared to be reading the form of service (Morning and Evening Prayer, Alternative Services, Series 3, Pew Edition); she read intently and as though it were not a booklet but a gripping novel. The children sang lustily, rather too lustily. Pity they don't get on with our two, Sue thought, it would have been handy, just across the road. Still, I'm not sure really . . . Just as well, maybe, one way and another. The rest of the casserole tonight, with some carrots, and I'll do an apple flan this afternoon. Lovely altar flowers, I wonder who did them?

*　　　*　　　*

'The Lord is my shepherd,' said George. 'I have everything I need. He lets me rest in fields of green grass and leads me to quiet pools of fresh water. He gives me new strength. He guides me in the right paths, as he has promised. Even if I go through the deepest darkness, I will not be afraid, Lord . . .'

And shifting his gaze from the top of the central pillar, there is Clare Paling staring at him, with what appears to be an expression of slight amazement, as though he were the intruder here, and not she.

*　　　*　　　*

The Coggan girls, stiff and smug with reflected glory, watched their father take his place at the lectern.

'The second lesson is from the first Book of Corinthians, Chapter Thirteen, verse one. I may be able to speak the languages of men and even of angels, but if I have no love, my speech is no more than a noisy gong or a clanging bell.

I may have the gift of inspired preaching; I may have all knowledge and understand all secrets . . .'

*   *   *

Sydney Porter, on his knees, said what he had always said and always would say. He rose, reached under his seat for the collection bag, and stepped into the aisle. As the voices of the congregation swelled with confidence and adjustment to the idiosyncratic timing of the organist, he moved from pew end to pew end, escorting the embroidered damask bag on its way down the church. Mrs Paling, he saw, was caught unawares, the Good News Bible in her hands rather than the hymnal, apparently reading and impervious to the bag until prodded by one of her children, whereupon she groped hastily in her purse and produced a note. There would be four notes, on average, the rest silver. The total would be between eleven and twelve pounds.

*   *   *

I beg your pardon? I *beg* your pardon? You did say Corinthians one thirteen? I did hear you correctly?

What has happened? Is nothing sacred? Where are sounding brasses and tinkling cymbals, for God's sake? What have they done, in the years of my unbelief, since at eight, and at ten, and at sweet sixteen and finally at sceptical eighteen, I last took part in this? Do we no longer trespass? Where are the paths of righteousness, and the valley of the shadow of death? In my childhood, I lifted up mine eyes unto the hills, I did not look to the mountains, and in what now appear to be those more enlightened times, the kingdom, the power and the glory were not yours but thine. God never told people to reproduce, he told them to be fruitful and multiply, as also did he create man in his own image, not to be like himself. What have they done, these people? Where is the majesty of language? Words were a matter for martyrdom,

75

time was. Have they exchanged a birthright for this mess of pottage?

* * *

The Palings, George uneasily noted, did not join the general exodus at the end of the service, but hung back. Mrs Paling appeared to be treating her children to a conducted tour of the church. Out of the corner of his eye, as he stood in the porch receiving the greetings of his flock (or, more frequently, their nods, grins or embarrassed avertings of the head) he could see her stooping before the font, pointing out the carvings, and caught, from time to time, a fragment of conversation. 'Why haven't they got any heads?' 'Because in the Civil War Cromwell's soldiers knocked them about.' 'Why?' 'Because they were saints.' 'Why didn't they like saints?' 'Because . . .'

'Nice day, Vicar.'

'I just thought I ought to mention, Mr Radwell, the Mothers' Union committee . . .'

'Turned out fine after all.'

'Good morning, Vicar.'

'Morning.'

'Say good morning to the vicar, Tracy.'

The Palings were now in front of the Noah window, down through which sunshine streamed, giving Mrs Paling a halo. A most inappropriate halo. She stood with a child at either side, the three of them rainbowed over with light filtering through Laddenham's last remaining fragments of medieval glass, patterned in blue and red and purple and gold by the figures of the prophets and the apostles and the whole company of angels and archangels. 'That's Noah in the Ark, letting the dove go,' said Mrs Paling. '*I* know the story of Noah's Ark, it's a good story.' 'So do I know the story of Noah's Ark.' 'And that is Cain, who killed his brother Abel.' 'Is that a good story?' 'It's an interesting story,' replied Mrs Paling, after a fractional pause. 'Why's that man holding half a baby?' 'It's a story called the Judgement of Solomon; that's an

76

interesting story too.' 'Do they all tell stories?' 'I suppose most of them do.' 'Are they true stories?' Mrs Paling's reply at this point, was inaudible. 'Stories don't *have* to be true stories to be good stories, do they?' 'No,' Mrs Paling agreed, 'they don't.'

'Ah, Vicar, I just wanted a word with you about . . .'

And so, at the point when at last Mrs Paling and her off-spring had done with the church furnishings, George was cornered by Miss Bellingham, and Mrs Paling was through the porch, with a 'Good morning' and a baring of those large teeth, before ever he could shake off the knotty problem of the outworn hassocks. And at the very moment when he had known suddenly what he could say, and how he would say it, and what it would lead to.

The church was empty now. He went into the vestry, where Sydney Porter was seeing to the collection money. He ex-changed a word or two with Sydney, removed his surplice, and went back into the main body of the church where, he saw, someone had dropped a glove in the aisle. He picked the glove up and stood holding it, a woman's glove, red leather with stitching. He said to Mrs Paling, ah, good to have you with us, and the children, splendid. Anna, isn't it? And Thomas. Glad to see you're exposing them to the temptations of belief (Mrs Paling at this point looked away, a touch embarrassed). No offence meant and none taken, I hope – I'm as broad-minded as the next man. Mr Paling not with us this weekend? Well, since you're all on your own, why not come back to the vicarage for a glass of sherry before lunch, I'm on my own too as it happens, we could have a chat about the restoration fund, to tell the truth there are one or two things I feel you and I might well sort out between ourselves before we involve the rest of the committee. And Mrs Paling, her expression of shy pleasure confirming the wisdom of this approach, replied that she'd love to, and yes, she'd been feeling they ought to have a private get-together sometime, what a good idea, thank you so much.

He stared in despondency at the blackened figures of Sir Peregrine and Lady Rushton, c. 1472, let into the floor of the nave, stylized and preserved for ever as a work of art in brass. All his life, it seemed to him, he had been addressing people who had already left the room. Always he had known what to do and how to do it slightly too late, ever since, as a boy, he had invariably grasped the rules of the game just as everyone else moved on to another activity. It did not seem to him likely, now, that he would change, or that the world would change to accommodate him. There were things of which he knew nothing; he read newspapers and books and watched the television and perceived waters into which he had never ventured. He had never been very happy or very unhappy; sometimes, as now, he knew a paralysing gloom, but suspected that there is worse. Once, he had been in love. At least, he had wanted desperately to go to bed with the girl and thought continuously of her, which fitted descriptions of the state. Mercifully, he discovered that there was already another man before he exposed himself to the humiliation of rejection. Now, he couldn't remember what she looked like.

He wished, sometimes, that he had married. Sex he would have enjoyed, and a wife would have been armour against the more aggressive female parishioners. He stood in the aisle, holding still the red glove, and pictured the wife he did not have; she swam into the rose window above the west door, a realistic figure, nothing like Mrs Paling, but dumpy and rather plain, wearing a brown raincoat and carrying a pile of organ music, not an arousing figure but a reassuring one.

Sydney, coming out of the vestry, had thought himself alone in the church until he saw the vicar standing there. He cleared his throat, not to make the man jump, but was ignored. He wondered if there was something wrong, the way Mr Radwell was staring at the rose window, but he couldn't see anything himself, just that frayed bell-rope that needed replacing.

He said, 'I'll be off now, then.' The vicar went on standing there, in the dusty sunshine; above him, the mottled plaster of the Doom painting, and all around the cluttered admonitions of the place – the symbolisms of the Creation and the Passion, of Noah and the Lamb and the Tree of Life, and the record of Laddenham's past, the naming of names, the Williams and Thomases and Elizabeths and Janes who were born and married and now rest, possibly, in peace.

Chapter Seven

Peter Paling, wearing one of five expensive suits he owned, sat on the sofa drinking a late-night whisky, talking of foreign parts and looking, his wife fondly thought, like a visitor in his own home. Between them, on the coffee table, in a luscious candy-striped wrapping, stood a very large bottle of scent. 'Thank you, darling,' she said. 'Lovely. That'll make them look even more askance at me in the next church appeal committee.'

'Ah. That. By the way what's all this about going to the Sunday service?'

'Anna has spilled the beans, has she? I told her she wasn't to stay awake for you.'

'She barely had. It was pretty incoherent. Something about someone cutting a baby in half.'

'They found biblical imagery engrossing.'

'So,' said Peter, 'it's not been too bad a week? I've missed you.'

'I've missed you too.'

'I had to have dinner with Belgian industrialists with awful fat wives. I even had to dance with one of the wives.'

'What sort of dance?'

'I don't know,' he said. 'What does it matter?'

'Sorry. It's the sort of detail that's interesting.'

'There are times, you know, when you can be faintly aggravating. You were meant to sympathize.'

'Oh dear. I am. I do.'

He re-filled his glass. 'Sometimes I feel you've got a bit detached. It worries me. I don't always know what you mean.'

'I've always been considered a bit odd,' said Clare. 'Surely you must have realized that? Your mother used to say I was too clever by half. Darkly. It wasn't meant to be flattering.'

'Oh well, so long as you love me.'

'I love you all right.'

Time was, she thought, in youth, one tried to explain oneself to people. One engaged in interminable tête-a-tête exchanges of self-revelation and analysis. Growing older, you lose both the knack and the inclination. I am devoted to my husband, but we are dissimilar people and too much mutual investigation might be a bad thing. I am periodically racked by insecurities; Peter is blessed with an untroubled spirit. We do not always experience things in the same way.

Soon after Thomas's birth the world had entered one of those phases of teetering instability when, for a matter of days or weeks, it seems as though catastrophe might well be the outcome. For others, albeit in far-away places, catastrophe was already there: nightly, on the television screen, rockets split the sky, people ran howling at the camera. Clare, sitting up in bed, the baby clamped to her breast, felt a sinking in her stomach; she looked down at Thomas's blue, milky, unseeing eyes and knew the awful responsibility of those who have created another being. And the awful apprehensions. Reading the newspaper, she said to Peter, 'What do you think?' 'What do I think about what?' 'About – the news. What will happen?' 'It'll be all right,' he said, and held out his cup for more coffee.

And it was. That time. For us, she thought, who have the luck to live where we do, to be what we are. Other places, other times – not so good. But for Peter, she saw, these spectral thoughts – guilts – had no place. And, seeing this, she realized one of the larger differences between people.

81

'I'm not detached,' she said, 'not in any way that matters, at least. Do you want to hear about my committee meeting? Not the most stirring occasion, but it had its moments.'

*   *   *

George, hastily tidying the vicarage dining-room in preparation for the committee, looked out of the window and saw Mrs Paling come up the garden path. Surprised and disconcerted, he glanced at the clock; three fifteen. The doorbell rang. He pushed the dustpan under the sofa and went to answer it.

Clare, following him into the empty room, said 'Gracious – am I the first? That's a change.' And then, 'It was for quarter past, wasn't it? Three-thirty? No wonder, then – sorry, how stupid, I can't have looked at the note properly. I'll come back.' She turned for the door.

'Don't. No need. Not worth it. Do sit.' He fussed round the sofa, patting it. As though, she thought, one were a dog.

'Oh, all right. But don't let me be in the way. Do get on with whatever you were doing.'

He hovered, interfering with rugs and cushions.

'I saw you,' he said, 'on Sunday. In church.'

'I saw you too,' she replied, amiably enough.

There was a silence.

'Hope you enjoyed the service,' he managed, at last.

She stared at him, incredulous. 'Enjoyed?'

'The flowers' – he rushed on – 'the altar flowers, I don't know if you noticed, the altar arrangement was done by Mrs Bradley, I wonder if you and your husband have met – Jennifer Bradley who lives at The Cedars. Miss Bellingham of course does the pulpit.'

'The flowers I didn't notice, I'm afraid,' said Clare. 'Sorry. I was more concerned with language.'

'Language?' His turn now to be taken aback.

'There seems to have been a clean sweep. The Authorized Version. The Book of Common Prayer. Out, I see. Superseded.'

'Ah, the new texts, you mean. The alternative services.'

'Those.'

He sensed danger. 'Younger people find them – um – find them more accessible. The old forms – all those long words, you know' – a laugh (you and I, of course, can cope with long words) – 'It's made it all more meaningful, putting things in a straightforward modern style.'

'Has it?' she said. 'Meaningful,' she went on, more to herself, he felt, than to him. 'Accessible.'

'Don't you think so?'

'Frankly, no.'

Grey eyes, looking at him: cool, dismissive. Small, neat breasts pushing against a red cotton shirt thing. Untouchable; poles apart; not for the likes of you. Fury swept him, all of a sudden. Fury and recklessness.

'I shouldn't have thought it would matter to you all that much,' he said, 'as a non-believer.'

She grinned, after a moment. 'Touché.'

He crashed on, emboldened. 'It's only words, after all.'

'Only words? *Only* words! Oh, dear. But you see, words are what I do believe in. They're all we've got.'

He stared at her. Very thin bony wrists; golden hairs on her arms; flat narrow thighs.

'And there are you people,' she went on, 'chucking out some of the finest words in the language. If you aren't to be trusted with that what are you to be trusted with?'

George snorted; he had intended a laugh, a sardonic laugh – what came out she could interpret any way she liked. 'What? It's just a question of modernizing, after all. There was a great deal that's not relevant to here and now and . . .'

'Oh, quite.' She was bored, suddenly: you could see that. Teeth flashed at him. 'Oh, I daresay, and I'm an intruder, in a sense, you've got a point there. Sorry, Mr Radwell.'

'George,' he began, 'do call me . . .' and the door bell rang, swamping him. Clare Paling got up, hitched a tight skirt down over that small behind, went to the table; outside,

Miss Bellingham trundled up the path, peering towards the window, hung about with shopping bags and cardigans.

At about four o'clock, the committee ran into trouble.

'All so *gloomy*,' accused Miss Bellingham. 'My goodness, people need cheering up these days, I would have thought – not harping on this kind of thing.' The account of the Swing riots and the shooting of the Levellers drawn up by Clare and Sydney Porter lay in front of her.

'I'm sorry,' said Clare. 'Mr Porter and I couldn't find a hilarious historic episode. They're a bit thin on the ground.'

Miss Bellingham sniffed. Once upon a time, thirty years ago, in Laddenham, you knew what to expect of a person by how they spoke and what they were; a woman like Mrs Paling would have been involved in certain, proper activities and you could have relied on her responses. For a long time now, things had been all anyhow; no wonder you got vandalism and illegitimacy.

'I fail to see how you're going to make a pleasant afternoon's entertainment out of this.'

Clare murmured something about the Tower of London.

'We took the boys there,' said Harry Taylor, 'year or so ago. Shocking entrance fees and queues half way down the road.'

Clare said she had meant it ironically. That the sufferings of others – especially if comfortably in the past – had proven drawing power.

'Well, I think that's a very cynical attitude,' said Miss Bellingham 'If you don't mind my saying.'

John Coggan intervened to point out that the format they were thinking of was not so much straight entertainment as some kind of broad-based event including several different things: a pageant, yes, probably, but exhibitions and displays as well. On the general theme of the church's history. A responsible, instructive programme.

Miss Bellingham, a little mollified, agreed that people like to feel they've learned something. 'I do myself. I don't think we should any of us feel complacent about what we know.

I'm studying Italian at the moment. And of course I'm very systematic about my reading.' Unlike, she thought, some. Only last week she had run into Mrs Paling in the public library with a pile of glossy-jacketed novels quite blatantly displayed in her shopping-basket. It told you a lot about a person, that sort of thing. One might well, of course, pick up the odd thriller oneself occasionally, but at least it would be discreetly popped underneath the travel and biography.

Silly old bag, thought Sydney Porter. He was surprised at the vehemence of his own irritation; he had, after all, endured Miss Bellingham, week in, week out, for many years now. The period when she had been People's Warden was particularly trying. It had been a great relief to see her unseated and her place taken by Jim Squires. He himself remained Vicar's Warden, and Squires was a great deal easier to work with. Miss Bellingham gave herself airs but when it came down to it she couldn't follow the basic rules of book-keeping. And she didn't know how to do decimal multiplication or division: he had noted that, at the time, with interest and silent contempt.

He leaned over to remind Mrs Paling of the plan they'd drawn up. Let her do the talking, she'd put it better.

George had spent the first half hour of the committee simmering down. He had very deliberately not looked at Clare Paling and concentrated on getting his colour back to normal and reducing his heart beat; you could do that, by sitting still and trying to think about nothing. Consequently, he had missed a lot of the proceedings. He became aware, suddenly, that Clare Paling was talking at some length, and he would have to listen. She seemed to have got it all worked out, this pageant business, or nine hundredth centenary celebration or whatever it was they ended up calling it.

'Nine hundred happy returns, eh?' said Harry Taylor. 'How about that, then?'

Mrs Paling thought not, on the whole.

Miss Bellingham was silent. The idea of the costumes

85

attracted her. If everybody was doing it you wouldn't feel silly, and that Quaker sort of dress, with those white caps, was very becoming.

'You won't get me into knee-breeches and a funny hat,' Harry Taylor went on heartily. 'Fancy yourself in a frock coat, Vicar?'

George said that it seemed an ambitious scheme, lot of work involved, not the sort of thing Laddenham was used to, bound to go down well though, he felt. He searched wildly for a telling contribution and came up, just in time, with some ideas about contacting the Tourist Boards and maybe the travel agents. Coachloads of Americans, that sort of thing. All the while he was talking there hovered before his eyes, ineradicable and exasperating, an image of Mrs Paling in one of those eighteenth century dresses out of which the bosom so engagingly spills. Except that Mrs Paling's wasn't the kind of bosom that spills. He substituted a sort of medieval page-boy get-up, very tight around the thighs; that was better.

'Had you finished, Vicar?' said John Coggan politely.

George jumped. They were all looking at him. Yes, he said, that was all, just thought he'd mention about the tourist possibilities, very good scheme, bound to pull in a lot of cash.

I am always maddened, Clare thought, by people whose speech is so inconclusive that nobody knows when they have finished what they have to say, least of all themselves. You'd think a man with the reassurance of the pulpit behind him could do better, instead of going off, apparently, into a trance. Visions of what? Not apocalyptic anyway, a more mundane bloke I never met.

'This re-enactment of the rioting business,' asked Harry Taylor, 'I take it we're not going to have them really chopping down the screen? Or jumping on the altar?'

Clare explained the scheme for spot-lighting different parts of the church, so that the action would seem to flit from one

86

part to another, probably with backcloths, and sound effects to replace actual destruction.

'I still think,' said Miss Bellingham, 'we should have maypole dancing.'

*   *   *

Sydney Porter slept badly, the night after the committee meeting. He lay long awake, and then sank into a lurid dream-racked sleep, one fantastic crazed sequence sliding into another. At one time there was a great noise in his ears, a crashing and a shattering, and he was in Mansell Road, a Mansell Road that crunched underfoot, that tinkled and sparkled as though strewn with Christmas decorations, and there was the Warden sweeping up broken glass – glass in splinters and glass in chunks and glass in fine dust that frosted the pavements and the front gardens. And he stood outside number forty-nine, where the windows gaped black and empty, and heard, as Mary and Jennifer must have heard, the crash of the glass blown in, and a roar, an awful irresistible roar – the one meant for them, the one with their name on it, nothing to be done, no way of escape, their number up. And he screamed in his sleep, soundlessly, his mouth open in the dark room, engines thundering outside along the Green.

In the morning, coming downstairs, he saw the broken fan-light above the front door with amazement. When he had fetched the dustpan and brush and carefully swept up the mess, he stood staring uneasily at the hole, through which a draught howled. The wind? A burglar? Neither made sense. He opened the door and saw, now, a further trail of destruction. Nearly all the newly planted young trees on the Green – some willows, a copper beech, chestnuts to replace the ageing ones – had been snapped off halfway down the stems. John Coggan was there.

'Did you hear them? Three or four in the morning, it must have been. That motor-bike gang. My God, if I'd known what they were up to I'd have been out like a shot.'

Sydney felt a curious lift of relief. The thing ceased to be personal; it wasn't meant particularly for him, it could have been anyone else. That mattered less, somehow. He indicated his broken window.

Later in the morning, the police came. 'Heaved a stone through it, did they?' said the young man, cheerfully. 'Bad luck.' Sydney, stolidly, gave such information as could be given. 'Do you know who they are?' The policeman shrugged. 'From Spelbury, probably, we'll have a look around.'

* * *

In the vicarage, Mrs Tanner stood at the window and surveyed the Green with relish. 'Now why do you think they'd want to do a thing like that, Vicar?'

George replied that he didn't know.

'On our estate, last year, there was some got a cat and put petrol on it and set light to it. Shocking, isn't it? Running about, it was, screeching, half-mad with the pain. I said to my husband, I think that's shocking. Shocking. And I don't care for animals, personally.'

The irritation that she set up in him was a tangible physical discomfort, like nettle-rash, or pins and needles. He felt it in the groin, at the back of his neck. He felt it as soon as she set foot in the house and it lasted until she departed again. At moments such as this it reached crisis proportions; he would have left the room, but it was his study, and he had a mountain of paper-work to get through and it was she who should be elsewhere in the house, not him. He said, 'Don't bother with this room, Mrs Tanner – it'll do till next time.'

She gave the windowsill a perfunctory swipe with a duster. 'I don't mind. I'll give it a go over all the same. You get on with whatever it is you're doing. Of course they won't get them, those boys, they'll never find out which lot it was.'

'I daresay not.'

'Dangerous, too, motor-bikes. My sister's boy came off his and broke his leg in two places, there was splinters of bone sticking through the skin, they say it'll never be quite right, only eighteen he is . . .'

George gritted his teeth. This could go on for some time. He took a fresh sheet of paper and wrote 'Dear Sir,' his pen scoring the paper.

'. . . just thought you'd like to know,' said Mrs Tanner. There was a note of grievance in her voice.

'Sorry?'

'Thought you'd like to know we were right, my husband and I, about it taking me out of myself, coming here twice a week. I'm feeling a bit of change. Thursday evening, I went along to the corner shop on my own. They're very surprised, at the clinic, they say they wouldn't have expected it.'

'Oh,' said George. 'Well, that is good. Splendid.'

'They broke the window of that Mr Porter opposite,' she went on. 'Shame. I stopped by to have a look on the way here, I had my daughter walk me that way instead of the usual. They cost a bit to fix, that type of glass.'

'Perhaps you could have done that on your own too,' said George nastily.

Mrs Tanner gave him a look of contempt. 'They say we can't expect miracles, at the clinic. They say it'll take time; time and patience. D'you want me to do anything more in here or is it all right if I have my cup of tea now?'

* * *

'Come here,' said Clare. 'Come here and sit down. I'm going to read to you.'

'Good–oh. Can we have . . .'

'No, you can't. We're going to read something rather different tonight.'

'That's the *Bible*,' said Anna, shocked.

'This, as you rightly point out, is the Bible. The Authorized King James Version, with which you are sadly unfamiliar. My fault, principally. I am a bad mother. You eat sweets between meals and go to bed at all hours and there are holes in your socks. But there is one thing I can try to put right. I can expose you to the language, like it or not.'

'The Lord is my shepherd,' she said. 'I shall not want . . . Stop fidgeting and take that gob–stopper out of your mouth . . . Yea, though I walk through the valley of the shadow of death, I will fear no evil: for thou art with me; thy rod and thy staff they comfort me.'

*　　*　　*

Keith Bryan, leaving the house in a hurry, did not notice the vandalizing of the Green. He had been one of the only residents who had refused to contribute to the Tree Planting Fund. 'Oh, come on,' Shirley had said, 'a pound or two, it's all they want, it's so embarrassing saying no.' 'Why the bloody hell should I? It's not my personal property, is it? What's it got to do with me? They can whistle for it – busybody Coggan and the rest of them.' 'Well, we all look at it, I suppose, the Green, and it's nicer with trees than not.' 'You can tell them to sod off,' he said sulkily, 'if they come back. You just want to get in with the other wives, that's all.' And they had had a row – no rare event – not that Shirley cared much more than he did, she was only trying to get a rise out of him. And it was a bloody nerve, these people expecting you to shell out for something that was basically none of your business. Like some new form of bloody income tax.

When Shirley told him about the vandalism he laughed. 'Well, that'll show them.'

'I think you're disgusting. Anything that doesn't affect you personally you don't care about.'

'That, my girl, is human nature, isn't it?'

He was in a glow of well–being. Debbie Comstock's perfume was on his hands still; there was a glittery hair on his lapel. Better get upstairs and have a clean up.

Shirley said, 'You might have said you wouldn't be back for supper.'

'I tried to ring – the phone must be on the blink again.'

'It's not the phone that's on the blink, it's you.'

He was half-way up the stairs. 'I don't have to answer to you for everything I do. So I went out for a drink?' He slammed the bathroom door. Below, he could hear her keening on.

The trouble was, he didn't know how serious Debbie was. Oh, she was saying and doing all the right things, but was it, when it came to the crunch, more than just a pretty heavy affair? He was going to have to find out – take the risk and find out – because he couldn't stand it like this much longer.

He washed and changed. It was that American series tonight, thank God, which would shut Shirley up for the next hour. When he was at the top of the stairs, he heard Martin's voice. 'Dad?' It was funny how you could clean forget about the kid, he'd always been a quiet, buttoned-up sort of boy. Keith went into the bedroom.

He was sitting up in bed, with a pile of tattered comics. 'Dad – it's the Air Show next week.'

'Is it?'

'Would you take me?'

'Yeah,' said Keith, 'O.K., then, why not?' He was filled with geniality, with generosity. Why not, indeed. Give the kid a smashing day out – it wasn't that often he took him any-where. He saw himself, in a flash, walking with Martin among the planes, explaining, instructing, the benign indulgent father, the boy hanging on his every word – 'Look, Martin, here's an old Spitfire Mark II, now the super-structure's interesting . . .' 'Gosh, Dad, fancy you knowing all about this kind of thing.'

'Will you honestly?' There was amazement in Martin's voice, and disbelief.

'Yes, sure, great – we'll have us a day out together.'

'The Red Devils are doing a display.'

'Good, good.'

The boy's eyes shone. 'Fantastic! Cor!'

'O.K., it's a date, then.'

'Promise?'

'Cut my throat,' said Keith cheerfully. He could afford a bit of largesse, feeling the way he did, Debbie only eighteen hours away, at the Black Horse at six, and later – well later they'd have to see about.

'Cut my throat and may I die. Good-night, kiddo.'

*　　*　　*

'Why do we have to go with you to Spelbury?'

'Because,' said Clare, 'there is food to be got and new shoes for you both and a business about the broken mixer. Come on, hurry up.'

Outside, Anna said with exaggerated concern, 'The *poor* trees. The poor baby trees, all spoiled. I think those naughty boys ought to be – ought to be *beaten*.'

'Ah. You're one of those, are you?'

'And they smashed Mr Porter's window,' Thomas put in.

'I know.'

'One of what, Mum?'

'Floggers and hangers. Never mind, love – you'll grow out of it, I trust.'

'Well, don't you? Think they should be beaten?'

'Not beaten, perhaps,' said Clare cautiously, 'but I agree it's thoroughly disgraceful.'

She opened the door of the mini, stowed the children away in the back, got into the driving-seat.

'Hey, what's that?'

There was something on the passenger seat. A creamy ribbon, some long rag of plastic, a burst balloon. She went to pick it up, touched for a moment its sliminess, recognized it, gave a yelp. The children leaned forward, interested.

Clare said, 'Oh, *Christ*!'

'What is it? What is that thing? Can I see?'

'No, you can't. It's nothing, some rubbish." She grabbed a hank of Kleenex from the parcel shelf, swept it up, deposited the lot in the bin, came back and cleaned the seat. The children were arguing now over territorial rights. 'Shut up, Tom – move over and give her some room.'

She drove to Spelbury, surprised at the sense of violation. Just because some bunch of yobbos . . . While one lay in tranquil, unsuspecting sleep. It was the sudden intrusion of lurking, dormant nastiness; as though the mud were stirred up. It was the stab in the back from that uncontrollable other world whose haunting presence on the fringes of bright reality it was never possible – or expedient – to forget.

Chapter Eight

Shirley Bryan seldom got out of bed before ten. What was the point? Martin could get himself off to school; Keith was poisonous in the mornings, they never exchanged a word anyway. She would lie frowsy in the curtained room, hearing the milkman's clink, passing cars, passing people. Quick, busy footsteps. She couldn't think what other people did with themselves: Sue Coggan, always on the go, off to the shops, baking, cleaning, bustling about. Her own days were cavernous with boredom, a long slouch from one hour to the next, with accompaniment by Radio One. The house was full of abandoned projects: half-finished garments, hexagons for patchwork cut out and then stuffed into a drawer, a junk-shop chest of drawers painted sparkling white until the paint ran out and it was too much of a sweat to go and buy some more. Occasionally she had tried evening classes: yoga, keep fit, upholstery. But dropped out, always, after the second or third time. She couldn't be bothered when something became an effort; it was always like that, the dress and skirt or whatever would run into difficulties, or the recipe would turn out more of a bother then she'd reckoned, or she'd just lose interest, cop out.

Today, she thought, lying there (the bed a bit smelly, the sheets needing a wash, curse it) she'd wash her hair and do it in a new style. Yes. Get a rinse maybe from Boots and try something really way out. The day took on some colour: yes, she'd do herself up nicely, give Keith a surprise, and finish off that pink shirt and wear it this evening. He wouldn't know what had hit him. And they'd go out for a drink.

She got up and ran a bath. Lying there in the steam, she thought of the night before. He'd been late – but he was always late, these days – and they'd had a row, of course. And in the middle of it he said, 'Christ, I wish I hadn't bloody well bothered to come back at all.' And her stomach plummetted; he means it, she realized, it could happen. But later it had all been all right again. He'd had a drink – given her one too, surprise, surprise – and they'd sat watching the telly together, first the new comedy series and then the news. On the screen, robed figures in some hot country were digging the bodies of children out of rubble: she said, 'That's terrible. Isn't that terrible, Keith?' and he nodded, and she thought, he's coming round, he'll snap out of it by bed-time, thank God for that. 'Another beer?' 'Yeah, thanks.' There would be sunny periods tomorrow, the forecast said, and temperatures around normal. She went out into the kitchen; it's O.K. really, she thought, I mean *really* everything's all right.

A blonde rinse? Or one of those coppery ones?

*   *   *

He said, 'My dad's taking me to the Air Show.'

'So's mine.'

'We're all of us going. Mum says I can take Steve.'

'I'm going,' Martin said, 'all on my own with my dad. We're having us a day out together. Just my dad and me. And he's going to tell me all about those old wartime planes and that.'

'There's going to be a Red Devil display. And there'll be a Phantom fighter.'

'Fantastic.'

'Brrrr – m! Brrrr – m!'

*   *   *

Clare said, 'Well, well, well.'

'What's up?'

'That car.'

'The Ford Capri?'

'That's it. What would you say the number was?'

'KJO 520S,' said Peter.

'That's what I think too. Well, well.'

'Could you,' he said kindly, 'expand?'

'That bloke I told you about, that charming fellow who boxed me in for two hours in a car park, is one of our neighbours. Isn't that nice? There he is setting off to work.'

He grinned. 'What are you going to do about it?'

'Nothing. Reserve it as an interesting piece of information.'

'And setting off to work is what I must do, too. Bye, love.'

'Bye. Incidentally, there was a used french letter on the passenger-seat of my car yesterday.'

'How the hell did that get there?'

'Someone,' said Clare coldly, 'bunged it in through the window, I presume.'

'You should lock the car. It'll get nicked one of these days, which would be even more inconvenient.'

*   *   *

The vicar had called in about the arrangements for the Saturday wedding. He hung on, chatting, while Sydney eyed through the window the only bright spell that morning and thought grimly he'd be lucky if he got in half an hour with the hoe.

'I was having a talk with Mrs Paling the other day about the new texts.'

Sydney said, 'Ah.' He watched cloud surge up behind the trees: mean, grey cloud.

'She's not altogether in favour. Interesting. Of course I've always had a few reservations myself, as I told her. There was a lot to be said for the old forms. But there it is – the Church has to move with the times like anything else. She took my point, I'm glad to say.'

96

Sydney made a noncommittal noise. He didn't much care for this new stuff himself, the old words were quite good enough as far as he could see, but it wasn't worth a lot of palaver and in any case where his own devotions were concerned he continued to say what he always had said. Radwell, though, was in a twitch for some reason. He stood there in the hall grinding the toe of his shoe into the carpet, making balls of fluff which would have to be swept up and going on about Series 3 and Mrs Paling and the Appeal Fund – which was a matter for the Appeal Fund Committee and not relevant at this moment. On the other side of the fanlight cloud was massing and darkening. George, following Sydney's glance, said, 'Ah – you got your window fixed.'

'Seventeen pound fifty,' said Sydney sourly.

George shook his head in condemnation and sympathy. He said again, twice, that he must be getting on, and did not. Outside, raindrops pattered. It came to Sydney, all of a sudden, that the vicar was a lonely man as well as one who could never be done with what he was saying or say what he meant to any effect. He seemed, standing there with his sandy hair and his pink face, like one of those diffident small boys who lurk on the edges of a playground, not invited to join in, while all around people are whooping and shrieking. Poor bastard, Sydney thought. It was one thing to have chosen that sort of life: another to have been shoved into it by circumstance. Because you were a bit of a ham-handed bloke with a silly laugh. It was one thing to have turned your back on involvement, quite another never to have known it. There he stood, in the murky subaqueous light of the hall, nattering on, while Sydney experienced a curious and uncomfortable combination of pity and patronage. Thus, once, in the war, he had watched the panic of a young officer during a sticky hour or two somewhere in the Red Sea, while he himself felt no fear: poor sod, he had thought, as he thought now, poor sod.

When the vicar had at last made an awkward departure Sydney fetched the dustpan and brush and tidied up the carpet.

It was gone twelve, and the rain looked set in. He went into the kitchen to put a couple of potatoes on for lunch.

There was another knock at the door. With a sigh, Sydney turned the tap off.

Shirley Bryan was standing there. She had a ravaged look to her, disconcerting, more blowsy even than usual. She said, 'I've come to ask you a favour, Mr Porter.'

He led her through to the lounge, where she would not sit but stood at the french window looking out at the garden. Words tumbled forth. Sydney, in embarrassment and apprehension, sat looking at the floor.

Her husband had left her this note. Another woman. He was clearing out; best thing. Sorry and all that.

She stood at the window, picking at the curtain with her fingernails. '. . . just stuck there all anyhow with some bills and stuff so I didn't see it till half way through the morning . . . Shock of my life . . . Rang the office but they said he's off north for three days on an assignment, wouldn't you just know it, they must have had it all worked out . . .'

Sydney cleared his throat and said something about a cup of tea. She ignored him.

'He says he's in love. In love! Fat chance I get to fall in love,' she went on, savagely now. 'Stuck here at home day in day out. Have an affair yourself, that's what they tell you in the magazines, show him you're attractive too. How do I get to have an affair, I'd like to know? When do I ever meet any blokes?' She ripped a loose thread from the curtain and twisted it round her finger. Sydney cleared his throat again and lined up the edges of the books on the table, to be appearing to do something. He felt as though some errant force were at large in the house – fire or flood or rampant rot. He wished she would go; he wanted no part of this. It was hard on her, yes, but he didn't see what he could do and other people's personal troubles are their own affair. Favour, she'd said. What favour? He shifted nervously in the chair.

'. . . so I rang my sister at her office and I'm going to go up to

London and stay with her for a couple of days, I can't stand it here all on my own in the house and she's got this bed-sit, I can think things out a bit, see what I'm going to do.'

Sydney nodded.

'But there's Martin, see.'

Sydney looked up in alarm.

'. . . so what I was wondering was could you do me a big favour – just keep an eye on him for a day or two till I get back. I can't take him, there's not room and anyway it'd be a bind, he'd get bored stiff and I want to be on my own. He'll be at school all day. It's just for him to know he can pop in here in the evenings a bit, see? I'd be ever so grateful. You needn't have him to sleep here, it's just so he knows there's someone handy if anything goes wrong.'

When at last she had left the smell of her cigarette hung in the room. He opened windows, emptied the ashtray, straightened the mangled curtain. There was a sense of invasion; the privacy of the house had been violated as tangibly as by the breaking of the hall window. In agitation, Sydney went into the kitchen to make himself something for dinner; in the process he smashed a plate. But what could he have said? No, Mrs Bryan, look after your own child, you've no business going off leaving a boy of that age on his own. He couldn't have said that. He'd had no option but to do what he did.

The boy didn't show up till nearly six. When he came he made Sydney jump, appearing like that suddenly at the french window. He must have climbed over the garden fence. He said, 'There was this note in the house.'

For a wild moment Sydney thought he was referring to the husband's note, then he realized the mother must have left another. She'd not even waited for the lad to come home, then.

'She said to come over here if I wanted.'

Sydney offered a meal, but the boy had already eaten. 'She left a pie. One of those frozen steak and kidneys you heat up. I had that. I'm not hungry. Can I look at your telly?'

Sydney, who would not normally have switched on at this time, nodded. Martin settled on the sofa, his knees hunched up to his chin; a peaky looking lad, Sydney thought, too pale, and those large grey sober eyes staring out. Presently, he left him there and went out to spray the tomatoes.

When he came back the programme had changed. Martin said, 'D'you watch this series, Mr Porter – it's good.' Sydney sat down; silly stuff, not something he'd have bothered with in the normal way, but after a minute he found himself smiling. The boy was grinning away; later, they laughed out loud, together.

At the end, Martin got up and switched off. 'There's nothing now.' He looked at Sydney, expectantly, it seemed. Sydney cleared his throat and looked away; it was only seven thirty. What time did a boy that age go to bed?

'She didn't say when my dad's coming back. He's taking me to the Air Show next week. Monday and Tuesday, it is.'

'Ah.'

'Monday, we'll go, I should think.'

Sydney got up jerkily and went over to the sideboard. He took out the biscuit tin and offered it. The boy chose a cream wafer. After a moment he said politely, 'I like chocolate ones best, actually.' Then, 'I watch you sometimes when you're digging your garden.'

'Ah,' said Sydney, again.

'You don't always know I'm there, I hide in the bushes.'

Sydney offered the biscuit tin.

'No, thanks,' said Martin. 'It's not spying,' he added, after a moment. 'It's just there's a place I use to hide in. If you don't like it I won't do it.'

Sydney looked at the boy. In ten years of neighbourhood, he realized, he had barely exchanged a dozen words with him before. He said, 'I don't mind. That's all right.'

'I like your garden. I like the way you've got everything in rows.'

'You've got to keep things under control, if you're doing veg.'

'My dad can't be bothered with gardening. Nor my mum.'

'No,' said Sydney.

They sat in silence for a while. Sydney got up and went to the corner cupboard. He got out a pack of cards. 'Like to learn how to play rummy?'

'O.K.,' said Martin with alacrity.

The boy picked up the game with ease. They had a couple of hands and then Sydney remembered the card tricks he'd known years ago. Martin crouched over the table in absorption. 'Cor . . . That's good . . . Can I have a go . . .'

Suddenly it was nine o'clock. Martin said, 'Shall we have the news?' Sydney got up. 'You switch on. I'll make us a cup of cocoa.'

In the kitchen, he stood looking out at the houses round the Green: each an island unto itself, each with the cosy inhabited glow of windows. He went back into the lounge. 'There's a bed upstairs in the back room. You could stop there tonight if you like.'

The boy's face lit up. 'Could I?'

Later, Sydney lay awake. He had not shared his roof with someone else for thirty-five years. For thirty-five years he had gone to bed, and risen again the next day, alone in a house. There was total silence: the boy might not have been there, he must have slept at once. Nevertheless his presence was absolute; it lent another dimension to the place. Sydney, disturbed, lay considering in the darkness, hearing the church clock strike midnight, and then the quarter.

*   *   *

George Radwell, making an entry in his desk diary, saw the year reach ahead in a progression of weddings and christenings, thick over the next few weeks, tailing off gradually into a barer autumn and winter. Funerals, of course, were disobliging, giving less notice. Backwards, the pattern repeated itself, clustered around weekends, weekdays yawning empty, a spate at Christmas and Easter and bank holidays. An endless vista

101

of smiling – or sober – faces; of people wearing clothes in which they did not feel quite themselves; of occasions detached from the normal for others but which, for him, were routine. 'Wilt thou have this woman to thy wedded wife . . . In the midst of life we are in death . . .' It had occurred to him once, staring down at the absorbed faces of yet another bridal couple, that his was an eerie presence at crucial moments in other lives: essential, yet irrelevant. There he stood, holding prayer book or cup of tea or glass of champagne, proclaiming or looking on or politely responding, while other people had emotions. The thought made him uneasy, lingering after the end of that particular ceremony; he had seen himself for a moment, walking back alone to the vicarage while chattering parties piled into cars.

Two weddings in succession on Saturday; a christening on Sunday. He turned to the post: electricity bill, brochures, church correspondence, a letter from his mother, passing a tetchy old age in Scarborough. She wrote on alternate Sundays. This letter, like most, dwelt on weather, rising prices, some domestic worry to do with plumbing or wiring, and included a mild swipe at George's deficiencies. A neighbour had dropped in flaunting a visiting grandchild: 'A lovely little fellow, what a pleasure he must be to them, well I suppose I must be grateful for what I've got. I'm doing you a grey pullover for your birthday, the same as last year's as the elbows will be out by now the way you wear them.'

It looked as though this line was to supplant her running commentary on his unmarried state which, over the years, had shifted from coy remarks about wedding bells to petulant criticism of his failure to 'settle down with a nice girl'. He had been a disappointment to her, he realized; mediocrity in childhood had been excusable, quite a good thing indeed – 'a good, quiet boy,' 'no trouble, we've a lot to be thankful for,' 'steady, not one of those temperamental ones.' But lack of performance in adult life was another thing; fortnightly, from Scarborough, she carped on.

He put the letter aside. The back door slammed with the force of a bomb blast, indicating the arrival of Mrs Tanner. George, hastily closing the desk top, prepared to flee to the church. Cornered in the hall, he had to listen to a protracted account of the death of a relative; through the window he saw the white mini, with Mrs Paling in the driving-seat, which prompted the usual unsettling feelings. 'You dropped your hankie, Vicar,' said Mrs Tanner heavily. 'Put it for the wash, shall I? It's very soiled.'

When he got outside the mini was the other side of the Green, stopped now, the window wound down, Mrs Paling talking to Sydney Porter. George, crossing the road, heading for the lych-gate, prepared and executed a wave of greeting (nonchalant, a little preoccupied, the gesture of a man with concerns of his own . . .) which neither of them saw.

*   *   *

'Poor little blighter,' said Clare.

Sydney, awkward and slightly agitated, continued. 'It's not that I'd choose to go round talking about it, I'm not a one for gossip.'

'I never thought you were.'

'It's the question of this Air Show.'

'I see the problem. It would be difficult for you because you haven't got a car . . .'

Sydney nodded.

'. . . whereas I have and as you've rightly guessed I'm taking my own offspring anyway – worse luck, I can't think of anything I need less than a day with a lot of roaring aeroplanes – and yes, of course I'll take him. A pleasure.'

'It'll be appreciated,' said Sydney stiffly.

'Well, it won't be much of a substitute, but it'll be better than nothing, I daresay.' There was a pause. Clare scowled at the car windscreen.

'What charming people. It makes the blood boil, doesn't it?'

Sydney cleared his throat and looked away.

'Sorry. I just meant . . . Anyway, it's good of you to keep an eye on him.'

'He's not a bother.'

'Let me know if there's anything I . . .'

'That's all right,' said Sydney quickly, 'we'll manage.'

Clare looked at him reflectively. 'She – the mother – she said she'd be back on Tuesday?'

'Thereabouts.'

'Hmn. Well, I'm glad you mentioned it. Tell Martin we're planning to have a picnic lunch on the way, and make a day of it, being as it's their half term.'

*   *   *

They had moved from rummy to whist, and thence to a game of Martin's unfamiliar to Sydney, called Attack. Cardboard armies, French and English (an archaism that struck neither of them as curious) confronted one another, hierarchies of generals and colonels and lieutenants and sappers and the all-powerful mine that could put paid to anyone, even the commander-in-chief. 'Attack!' 'Private.' 'I'm a major. Your go.' 'Attack!' 'Mine!' 'Bother, that was my last general.' They watched the telly. Sydney made a treacle tart, resuscitating a long forgotten skill. Under a watchful eye, Martin learned to wield a hoe, to distinguish a carrot from a weed. From time to time, he drifted back to his own house, returning on one occasion to say, 'My mum telephoned.' 'Ah.' 'She said she'd been trying on and off for ages, she said she was getting ever so worried.' 'Did she, now?' said Sydney coolly. 'Anyway, she said thank you ever so much for letting me come over here and it's O.K. if I go on sleeping in your house. She said she may stop up in London with Auntie Judy till next week, since I'm getting on fine on my own.' After a moment Martin added, 'She didn't know about dad taking me to the Air Show, he's gone off somewhere for the firm, she doesn't know when he'll be back.' 'Ah.' 'He forgot, I suppose.' 'I been thinking,' said Sydney, 'there's that old shed on the far side of the potting-shed, that I don't use, we could clear that out and you could have it for somewhere of your own, keep your junk in it, like.'

*　　　*　　　*

'I'm happy!' cried Anna. 'I'm so happy I could *scream*!'

'Let's scream, then.'

'Go on, Thomas!'

'You first.'

Anna gave a ladylike shriek. 'Now you.'

'Maybe not,' said Clare, 'I might upset the cows.'

The picnic site, unlike most picnic sites, had indeed turned out a perfect selection. It was by the river, near the spot at which Clare had seen the Red Devils. They sat on luxuriant grass intricately woven with wild flowers; the water, a few yards away, was dappled with light that filtered down through alders and willows. There was birdsong and faint mysterious ploppings along the river bank, and a smell of hay.

'Can we start the ice cream now?'

The flowers sparkled: yellow and blue and mauve and crisp white. Examined closely, at eye level in the forest of the grass, their arrangement was of wonderful complexity, a labyrinth of growth, stems twisting and spiralling, swarming under and above, an anarchic but ordered world in which everything struggled for light and air and achieved a mindless perfection in the process: the glint of buttercups against a misty under-growth of speedwell, a bright tangle of stitchwort pierced by mauve pinnacles of bugloss. Elaborate, disorderly and beautiful.

The children, replete, flung themselves down: Anna and Thomas on their backs, Martin a few yards away leaning against a tree-stump. He had been quiet, polite, a little with-drawn before the exuberance of the younger two.

'Sure you wouldn't like some more, Martin?'

'No, thank you.'

The bodies of children, Clare thought, have the same grace

as plants: they sprawl and reach and bend, they help themselves to the atmosphere, to light and warmth and nourishment. They neither posture nor contrive; they are unconcerned: they are a delight to the eye. How curious, and how significant, that of the many ways in which one loves one's young, the physical should be one of the most forceful: the feel of them, the look of them.

At such times as this, at such transcendent moments when in a suspension of time all is actually right with the world, it is the feel and the look of things that manifest that rightness: the marvellous presence of the physical world, impervious and uncaring, but to which nevertheless one turns for exaltation. The sky, on a day like this, is deeper, the clouds more lavish, the touch of the sun on my arm more sensual. Colour is more intense: the flowers, the grass. Sound is more complex: the river, the birds.

Thomas rolled over, heaved a sigh. 'I like this place. Can we come here again?'

'It's *lovely*!' said Anna theatrically. 'It's so beautiful. Don't you think it's beautiful, Mum?'

'It is. Yes, it certainly is.'

'When I see anything beautiful like those flowers I feel a bit weepy, don't you?'

Thomas, maddened by this display of sensibility, sat up and began resolutely popping bubble gum.

'Well,' said Clare with caution, 'that's pushing it a bit, perhaps.'

'*Stupid*!' snarled Thomas.

'Shut up.'

'Shut up yourself.'

'Enough, both of you!'

Anna was now leaning cosily against her mother, in exclusion of the lumpen male element. 'Mrs Driver at school says things being so lovely, flowers and snow and mountains and everything, proves there must be a God.'

'Does she now.'

'Don't you think she's right?'

'Frankly no. Both wrong and unoriginal.'

'If I was God,' said Thomas, 'I'd make a cow-pat, an absolutely enormous cow-pat, and push Mrs Driver in it.' He howled with mirth.

Anna threw him a withering glance. 'He's torn his new T-shirt, Mum. Mrs Driver says the world couldn't just be like that by itself. What do you think, Mum?'

'Perhaps,' said Clare tersely, 'Mrs Driver would like to explain in that case why He also allows people to fall off lovely mountains and kill themselves, or die of cold in the beautiful snow.'

'Or eat poisonous plants and get horrible agonies and die,' added Thomas triumphantly. 'Some berries are deadly poison, they burn away your insides and you scream and scream and die.'

'True,' said Clare, 'if a bit over-dramatic.'

Anna, affronted, had removed herself and was picking flowers. She examined a sprig of forget-me-not with exaggerated reverence, and glared at Clare and Thomas. 'Well, I don't care if you don't like the flowers. I'm going to take them home and put them in water and give them to Daddy when he comes back.'

'I do like them,' said Clare, attempting appeasement, 'I think they're lovely. Just I don't think they have anything to do with God.'

'Nor do I,' said Thomas, closing ranks. 'Silly old God.'

Clare began to pile the picnic debris into the basket. 'That'll do. And don't talk like that – it's a serious matter, as it happens. Come on, we'd better be moving.'

In the car, Anna said, 'How far is it to the Air Show? How long till we're there?'

'Not far. About twenty minutes or so.'

'Hurray!'

Clare could see, in the mirror, their faces, lined up in a row; eager, glowing faces. Martin, too, looked animated now, excited. She said, 'You'll have to tell me all about the aeroplanes, Martin – I'm dead ignorant about that sort of thing.'

'O.K.!'

'I want to see a Spitfire. And a Hurricane.'

'A bi-plane.'

'The Red Devils!'

'Isn't it exciting!'

'Let's all sing!' cried Thomas.

'Right you are. What shall we sing?'

'Ten green bottles,
Hanging on the wall.
Ten green bottles,
Hanging on the wall.
Then if one green bottle,
. . . You too, Mum . . .
Should accidentally fall,
There'd be nine green bottles,
Hanging on the wall.'

'Drive *fast*, Mum!'

Now, now, she said, we mustn't let things go to our heads. Their discordant voices shrilled in her ear. 'Move a bit, Tom, I can't see out of the back window'; a grey ribbon of road vanished under the white nose of the mini and unreeled again behind. 'Nine green bottles, hanging on the wall.' Oh, the exuberance of children! Well, there's nothing like spreading a little happiness. '. . . if one green bottle . . .' Cow parsley brushed the side of the car. 'Isn't it a lovely flowery road, Mum!' 'A lovely narrow road, too.' Sharp bend – I'll say – good and sharp.

Christ!

The decision, if that is what it can be called, is instinctive rather than considered. Hurl the car to the left, anything rather than meet head-on the thundering maw of the lorry. Stupid bastard, stupid murderous *bastard*. Plunge the mini into the grass, the cow parsley, the meadowsweet . . .

A jolting, sliding stop. A sickening lurch. Christ, will it go right over?

Keep calm. Switch the engine off.

She said, 'Anna?'

'Yes.'

'Tom?'

'What?'

'Martin?'

'I'm O.K.'

If they can all speak, she thought, then it is not too bad.

Chapter Nine

'. . . and we were all in a heap on the floor, Tom's elbow was in my *eye*, the car tipped right over almost on its side and there was broken glass, Mum had a cut on her leg, and the front was all bashed in.'

'. . . and we went in the police car, a real Panda car . . .'

'. . . and the lorry driver gave us some chocolate.'

'As well he might,' said Clare tartly. She felt, suddenly, exhausted. Anything to get indoors and into a hot bath. Not to stand here talking to the neighbour though he means well, I'm sure, the solicitude is quite genuine.

George Radwell was clucking away. 'He was on the wrong side of the road, I suppose?'

'That's right.' Poor man, one ended up feeling a bit sorry for him, the lorry driver, for goodness sake – white as a sheet and more shaken than we were, if anything.

'And they were measuring the road with tape-measures . . .'

'. . . and we couldn't go to the Air Show at all. And a truck came with a crane and just picked Mum's car up, just like that!'

'Come on,' said Clare, 'enough commotion for one day. Thanks, Mr Radwell – no, honestly, there's nothing you can do, everything's taken care of. Thanks all the same, bye.'

Later, the children in bed, when she was sitting at last with her feet up on the sofa, a drink and a book in hand, the telephone rang.

There were cracklings and sighings, then Peter's voice: distant, going on about thank goodness, you're all right then, I've been worried.

'Look,' she said, 'are you suddenly psychic or something? What is all this? How did you know? In the *evening paper*? Peter, just what is it that you think might have happened to us today?'

He was clearer now: she could hear what he said.

She took a long, deep breath: explained.

'Are you there, Clare?'

'Yes, I'm here.'

'Well, thank goodness you never got to the thing.'

'How many people,' she said, 'were killed?'

'About half a dozen, I think. And injuries. Some children, I'm afraid. Ghastly. Well, look, love, I'm tremendously relieved. Look after yourself. And I'll see you on Friday.'

*   *   *

'Those red aeroplanes,' said Mrs Tanner, 'that do the displays. They say it came down just like that. Ploughed into the fence and the people that were standing there. The radio said a few yards more and it would have been dozens. It makes you think, doesn't it? They say there was the most terrible screaming. The children, see. And there was the debris flying in all directions, there was one woman got hit nearly five hundred yards away, a chunk of metal split her arm from the shoulder to the elbow. There's three in the intensive care still, the radio said – no, four I think it was. Terrible, isn't it? My sister-in-law was there, but they were over the far side. They saw it come down, though. Afterwards they tried to get nearer – to see the wreckage and that – but the police had it all cordoned off, they said you couldn't get anywhere close. I said to my husband, good thing I wasn't there, with my nerves. And we'd thought of it, now I'm getting out so much more. There was a little girl

111

of three, you know. Shame. It was on the news – but of course you've not got the TV, have you Mr Radwell? We saw it on BBC and then we switched over – they had more pictures on ITV.'

*   *   *

Sydney Porter, also, watched the BBC news. When it was over he turned the set off and sat staring at the blank screen, filled now with sights he would rather not have seen. The boy was in bed, upstairs; he had come back tired, eaten ravenously, and gone up. The mother had telephoned to say she would be back tomorrow. Sydney thought of those aeroplanes, slicing the sky above his vegetable garden that day; he heard that invasive, inescapable noise. He heard other inescapable noises, in other places, at other times. At last he sighed and went into the kitchen to tidy up for the night.

Later, he looked into the room in which the boy was sleeping – cautiously, not to wake him. In the shaft of light from the door Sydney could see his clothes flung down on the floor, the hump of his body in the bed. The curtain billowed in a gust of air; Sydney stood hesitant, concerned suddenly about draughts; eventually he tiptoed across the room and closed the window a little more.

*   *   *

Martin dreamed he was running through grass, thick grass that snatched at his ankles, in flight from something unseen, something enormous and bestial that snuffled after him. And the grass grew thicker, thicker and longer, it was like trying to run in water, his limbs dragged, he was panting, he ached with the effort, and all the time the thing got closer. And then he knew suddenly it was a dream, and all he had to do was claw his way back to reality. But he couldn't do it; he struggled to wake, and the dream clutched him, dragged him back, fought to keep him.

And then he was out of it, sitting up in bed gasping, as

112

though he really had been running, too hot, sweat trickling under his pyjamas. And the bed felt funny, and the bedclothes, he thought in panic he must be in another dream until he remembered it was Mr Porter's spare room bed, that was where he was.

He lay down, and the dream receded. Mum was coming back tomorrow, he wouldn't be sleeping here any more. She sounded funny, on the telephone; when he'd asked her where Dad was she'd said something he didn't quite hear. And when he said, 'What?' she'd said never mind, and started on about Auntie Judy and how they might go for a holiday in Spain, with her and her boyfriend and this other man Auntie Judy knew.

He was glad she was coming back. He didn't like the empty house; when he was there it seemed to crouch around him, hostile, the silence thumping in his head. It was all right here, at Mr Porter's. Mr Porter was nice. He hadn't known he was nice; before he'd just been someone you saw, he was neither nice or nasty, he just was, that was all there was to it.

He felt a bit sick. He often felt sick, and he had that knotty feeling in his stomach a lot of the time now.

*　　*　　*

'How awful about your car! But wasn't it a miracle you weren't any of you hurt, you must feel it was your lucky day, in a way, and then not getting to the Air Show. Of course I suppose the odds are you wouldn't have been anywhere near the crash anyway, but it makes you think doesn't it? Tracy, don't drag like that, I'm talking to Mrs Paling, be quiet. I could hardly believe it, when it came on the news. I mean, you don't expect things like that on your own doorstep, do you? It made me feel quite funny for a minute. All *right*, Tracy, I'm coming.'

*　　*　　*

Clare stood at the window. The world, on this summer day, was blue and green, sky above and rich pushing growth below,

113

the showering willows of the gardens opposite, the shaggy laden chestnuts, the bright trim grass. Outside, in her own garden, the children played. It was still half term. They had been joined, this morning, by Martin. Yesterday's events had, it appeared, initiated a relationship of some kind between him and Thomas.

Sue Coggan came out of her house, set off briskly for the shops. George Radwell crossed the road, went through the lych-gate and up the churchyard path. Sydney Porter opened his front door and set about sweeping his steps.

A red Ford Capri, registration number KJO 520S, drew up outside the Bryans' house.

Clare moved closer to the window, more central, continued to observe.

Keith Bryan got out of the car, sorted keys, opened his door, went in. Came out, three minutes later. Stood, for a moment, hesitant. Caught sight of Sydney Porter.

Clare lit a cigarette. Watched Sydney and Keith Bryan talk, saw Sydney's gesture in the direction of her house, sensed his distaste for the man, noted the renewed vigour of his sweeping. Watched Keith Bryan cross the Green, approach her own front gate.

She opened the door. 'Well, well. We meet again.'

'Eh?'

Agreeable, to see the jaw drop (they do, at least not so much a drop as a sideways shunt). Interesting, the visible process of a man first nonplussed, then shocked into remembrance, then massively disconcerted.

'We meet,' said Clare, 'again. My car, fortunately, is not around at present. How's yours? Which I so vividly recall.'

He looked slantwise over her shoulder, licked his lips. 'Look, it was all a bit of a mess-up, that. You caught me on a bad day. I didn't know you lived in Laddenham, either.'

'That would have made a difference?'

'You know how it is, you get a run of things going wrong, someone needles you . . .'

114

'Oh, quite,' she agreed, 'and naturally you feel the urge to pass it on.'

He shifted his gaze over the other shoulder, sullen now. 'Look, no hard feelings? Sorry about it. You had a point.'

She beamed. 'I did indeed. And now, I take it, you've come for a word with your son.'

'That's right.' He was all confidence and confidentiality; matey, back on his feet. 'The thing is, I've got to take off up north for a week or two – business assignment that's cropped up. Truth to tell, it may last longer than that, there's chat about a promotion, between you and me. So with Shirley having to pop up to town to see her sister, old Sydney Porter next door's been keeping an eye on the boy, apparently. And he told me he was over here with your two, so I thought I'd just look in and tell him goodbye in case I do stop up in Liverpool for a while.'

She held the door open. 'You'll find him in the garden,' she said coldly. 'Down those steps.'

When he returned she was in the sitting-room. He put his head round the door. 'Cheers. I'll be off now. Too bad about your smash, by the way – I hear you never made the Air Show.'

'Martin,' she said, 'had been looking forward to going to it with you.'

'Ah. Yes. Pity about that. It wasn't on, as things turned out.' He glanced round the room. 'These older houses look quite good when they're done up, don't they? Not a bad investment. Personally I prefer a modern development like we're in but I must say you've made something of this.'

She stared at him.

'Yes, well, I'll be off then, as I said. Cheers.'

She watched the Capri drive off and went out into the garden. 'Listen I'm going over to the church to see about this lighting for the pageant. You can stay here if you're sensible. Martin – you're in charge, as eldest. See they don't do anything silly.'

He nodded, pleased.

'I'll be back in half an hour or so.'

Crossing the Green, she thought it odd that she was finding this whole ridiculous pageant business stimulating. Her own role had become that of practical woman and entrepreneur – negotiating with electricians about how to provide spot-lighting for the various features of a building only minimally equipped with electricity, tracking down and sorting out hirers of costumes, synchronizing the activities of others. The actual devising and production of the dramatic episodes had been handed over to a local lady with pretensions in the world of amateur theatricals. Casting sessions had already been held; enthusiasm had been gratifyingly – and perhaps surprisingly – high. There was competition for starring roles, and offence taken. There were complaints about the paucity of good female parts. Miss Bellingham, with satisfaction, pointed out that she had already said it was the wrong kind of history to have chosen; 'Elizabethan, or Restoration, and you could have had maids of honour and dancing and the little girls in pretty frocks. But of course Mrs Paling and Mr Porter were set on the depressing side of things.' Clare retorted tersely that history had this tendency to be both male-dominated and short on happy endings. Miss Bellingham, with a sniff, turned her attention to promoting discord between rival contestants for the part of the Cromwellian colonel responsible for the Leveller executions. The successful candidate, in the end, aptly perhaps, was a local butcher. In a determined attempt to introduce a feminine interest he had been provided with an historically unauthentic wife pleading for clemency, a role undertaken with panache by the barmaid from the Crossed Keys, a popular piece of casting. The parts of the three Levellers were won by a young master from the primary school, the dentist, and the newsagent's son. Enthusiasm to play the nineteenth century landowner against whom the Swing riots were directed rather hung fire until the splendours of the costume were pointed out: then, after brisk competition, the part went to Ray Turnbull, proprietor of the hairdressing salon in the High Street, Giuseppe of Rome.

The committee, naively perhaps, had had the notion that it might add piquancy to the event to have the rioters played by actual descendants of the transported men, if such could be found. George, familiar with the parish register, pointed out that in two instances the names were still around: a Karen Binns had married only last year, a Wayne Lacy had been christened at Easter. But no one auditioning for the parts claimed or indeed would own to, descent. It was Mrs Tanner who remarked succinctly that you couldn't expect them to, could you? This comment had been reported to Clare who, disturbed, had taken the subject up with her, standing on the pavement outside the vicarage. The point is, she explained, that yes, they were technically criminals, but nobody feels that nowadays; today people feel they were entirely justified, they were more or less starving, sympathies have swung in quite the other direction, it's an ancestry to be proud of, I'd have thought. Mrs Tanner, staring at her as though at an evangelical preacher of some feckless sect, remarked with unswerving cynicism that there was no smoke without fire, and you couldn't expect people to do other than keep quiet about something like that.

Clare's visit to the church this morning was to check on numbers and positioning of spot-lights before inviting estimates from a couple of local firms. She stood in the aisle, holding clipboard and a rough plan, making notes and trying to work out distances. Dust tumbled in shafts of sunlight; a stone mask of entirely pagan inspiration grinned down from a capital; the mythology of two thousand years glowed from the nave windows. And furthermore, she thought, ridiculous as it may be, I am more than happy to do my bit for such a place. Prop it up for a while longer. Entirely, of course, according to my own unbelieving lights. A double spot above that pillar, to cover the pulpit and the Doom painting, singles each side of the nave, one in the chancel for the altar . . .

117

George Radwell's voice made her jump. 'What? I didn't realize there was anyone there.'

'I said, anything I can do to help?'

'No, no. I'm fine.' She wished he wouldn't stand right by her like that, breathing. Admittedly, people have to breathe.

'Good of you,' he said, 'to get so involved.'

'Not at all. I'm enjoying it.'

He padded behind her. 'Not being a churchgoer yourself.'

'I've got a feeling,' she said, 'we've had this conversation before. Perhaps you'd just hold the end of the measure for a minute. Does it matter if I stand on the pew?'

Her breasts, thus, were at eye level, less than an arm's reach away. The shirt thing, as she stretched upwards, came out of the waist of the skirt, leaving a strip of bare skin. She looked down; he stepped back.

'Please don't bother. I can quite well do this on my own. I'm sure you're busy.'

She made him think of gooseberries. When he was a child he had never known if he loved them or hated them; that acid compelling taste, the way they furred your mouth. He didn't know if he wanted to hit her or grab her. She was sitting now, scribbling on her pad; he was dismissed.

What's wrong with the man? she thought. Trailing around, when he can't stand me.

'No after effects I hope?' he said. 'The accident.'

'Absolutely none, thanks.'

'It shakes you up a bit.'

'It does indeed.'

'Some people might feel like offering up a prayer.'

'I daresay they might.'

He had had another of those dreams about her, the night before. The same sort of stuff: knickers and writhings and then suddenly she'd just got up and walked off. Laughing.

He had a rush of blood to the head. 'I don't see how you people explain that kind of thing. A deliverance of that kind.'

'It doesn't seem to me,' she said, 'to require explanation.'

118

'The world isn't that haphazard.'

'Some people feel it is precisely that.' She got up, determinedly. Please, she thought, don't go on. The awful thing is that I realize now, and you are not dreadful, but sad. Please stop.

He crashed on, booming in the silence. 'The hand of God . . .'

She stood still. 'Mr Radwell. George. If the hand of God twitched my car out of the way of that lorry yesterday, then it also threw an aeroplane on top of six other people including a three year old child and a pregnant woman. If there is someone around who does things like that, then I want no part of whoever or whatever he, she or it may be.'

George?

'I believe,' she said, 'insofar as I believe anything, that we are quite fortuitously here, and that the world is a cruel and terrible place, but inexplicably and bewilderingly beautiful.'

George.

'And I believe that people are capable of great good and great evil, and ought to be good. And I believe that the capacity for love is the greatest we have. Every kind of love. Kindness or charity or tolerance or whatever you care to call it.'

'You sound like a Christian.'

'Oh no. Because I believe that when we die we die and that is that. And I also believe in language.'

Syndey Porter came into the church and saw the vicar and Mrs Paling at the far end. They were standing face to face and for a moment he thought they were having some sort of an argument. Mrs Paling made a remark he didn't catch, and then the vicar snorted that silly laugh of his and said something about Christian and then Mrs Paling spoke again and then they just stood there as though they'd got to stalemate. Sydney, embarrassed, cleared his throat; he didn't want to be a witness to anything that might be better not witnessed, nor did he want to get drawn into any kind of discussion of religious

119

things, if that was what they were talking about. He hadn't thought Mrs Paling a religious person, though, and Radwell wasn't given to talk of that kind except in the line of duty, as it were, confirmation classes and sermons, and his sermons weren't what you might call particularly theological.

They heard him and turned round and he saw now that the vicar was very red in the face and Mrs Paling looked put out. But she pulled herself together quickly and began talking about the electrical problems, and presently the vicar muttered something about things to see to and went away. Mrs Paling then asked about Martin and if he'd seemed upset by the accident at all, and referred to his father turning up just now. She didn't care for him, that much was obvious.

'He could always sleep over with us, you know. He and Tom seem to be very thick at the moment.'

'No need,' said Sydney quickly. 'It's no bother.'

Mrs Paling looked at him and nodded. 'Fine, I'd better get back.'

Sydney tidied up the vestry and did a round of the churchyard, removing three coke tins and some crisp packets. It was hot and sunny and there were wild flowers in the rim of long grass around the untended graves at one side – the older gravestones whose inscriptions were nearly indecipherable. A pink climbing rose showered down the wall. Butterflies danced above the buddleia in the corner. It would have been a pleasant place for a nice sit down on a bench with a newspaper; there was something companionable, cosy, even, in the carven names all about. But once he had come in the early morning in winter during a heavy snowfall and it had seemed a place of the utmost desolation. He had stood just here, by the lych-gate, with the tombstones in front of him, ranks of blunt shapes capped, each, with white, the snow thick underfoot and falling still, unstoppable, part of the inevitability of things, shrouding all trace of life, no footsteps, no sounds. And the tombstones had been like observant presences, gaunt and waiting; he had felt as though he were faced by the dead themselves, as though he alone stood warm in a cold world, as though he were watched and warned. And for a few minutes he had experienced loneliness as seldom before – as seldom since those weeks and months in 1941 – he who rarely sought company, who could manage nicely on his own.

Back in the house, he took from the fridge a packet of frozen beefburgers and studied the cooking instructions with a mixture of perplexity and suspicion. The boy had said they were his favourite thing. He consigned them to the frying-pan and put another pan on for chips. Peas from the garden were already prepared and ready to cook, and carrots too, plenty of good fresh veg might get him looking a bit less pasty.

Sydney set the table: knives and forks, spoon for the boy's ice-cream, bottle of this Corona stuff he fancied. The beefburgers sizzled promisingly; there was a good smell of minty peas. In the normal way of things he wouldn't bother so much about a hot meal in the middle of the day, but a growing lad needed it. He put a couple of plates under the grill to warm, checked the table, looked out of the window and saw Martin crossing the Green; it would all be nicely ready as he came in.

Chapter Ten

She had new clothes on and she'd done something funny to her hair, it had streaks in it and looked tidier. She'd brought him a model aircraft kit and a Blue Peter Annual.

She kept on about Dad. When had he come? Did he go in the house? What did he say? There was an edge to her voice; she didn't say 'Dad', she just kept talking about 'him'. Martin felt as though he were in some dark room with murky shapes you couldn't quite make out, presences you'd rather not know about. It was worse than lying in bed hearing them shouting at each other. He said, 'What's wrong, Mum? Why's Dad gone away? He will come back, won't he?' She went upstairs and when he followed her she snapped at him not to trail around after her, it got on her nerves. Later, from the garden, he looked towards the house and saw her face at the window, and it was all screwed up and red, as though she were crying. But she couldn't be, grown-ups don't cry. After a while he climbed over the fence to Mr Porter's and played in the shed that Mr Porter had cleared out for him. Mr Porter was going to put some shelves up when he could get hold of some wood, so he could set up his models there. Mr Porter said maybe there'd be a bit more space than back in his own room. It was true, there would. Actually, Martin realized, Mr Porter hadn't ever seen his room, he'd never been into their house, which was funny since he'd always lived next door. Martin didn't think he'd want him to, in fact; it would be embarrassing, somehow.

The house was all right again now she was back, it didn't lurk any more, it hadn't that frightening empty feeling. In the evening, when they were watching telly he said, 'You aren't going to go away again, are you, Mum?' She was eating a chocolate (she was always eating chocolates, since she came back, she kept saying, 'Christ, I'll get so fat,' and then she'd reach for another). She didn't answer for a minute and then she said I dunno, maybe, I've not thought really, maybe we might go for a holiday in Spain with Auntie Judy, that'd be nice, wouldn't it? 'And Dad?' he said, 'when Dad comes back, d'you mean?' She didn't answer. Have a choc, she said, holding out the box, go on, before I hog them all.

School would start again tomorrow. He didn't suppose he and Tom Paling would be friends at school, you couldn't really, with Tom only being seven and a half. But he hoped they'd go on playing at home, it was better than being on his own. The Palings' house was funny: it was all bright and light and Mrs Paling sang when she was doing the washing-up, songs he'd never heard of, not pop, peculiar songs. And she talked to Anna and Tom – and him, come to that – in a funny way, as though they mattered, as though they weren't just children. He wasn't sure if it was embarrassing or nice.

*   *   *

Sydney washed up the breakfast things: one bowl, one plate, one cup and saucer, knife, teaspoon, teapot. He saw Martin go past, heading for school; he saw the Paling children scurry across the Green; he saw Sue Coggan pausing to adjust a daughter's drooping sock. He swept the kitchen floor, ran the vacuum over the hall and the lounge. Then, it being overcast but fine, he went out into the garden: carrots to be thinned, hoeing, some rough edges that needed a going over.

Half way through the morning Shirley Bryan appeared at the fence. 'Thanks ever so much for keeping an eye on Martin.'

Sydney inclined his head. 'That's all right.'

'No, I mean it, it was really kind. It took a weight off my mind, I can tell you.'

Sydney made a vicious stab with the edge-trimmer.

'I said to my sister, well, one thing, I don't have to worry about Martin, with Mr Porter being so kind. He'll be all right.'

Sydney, his back half-turned, shovelled loose earth and grass roots into the trug. He lined up the string against the edge and stabbed downwards once more.

'At that age,' said Shirley Bryan, 'they don't take in a lot, do they? Just as well. I'm feeling a bit better in myself now, I'm sleeping all right and frankly if Keith walked in this minute I'd as likely give him a clip about the ear as burst into tears. My sister said, look, Shirley, face up to it, you've been at each other hammer and tongs for years now, this has been coming for a long time, let him go off with his fancy piece and good luck to him . . .'

Sydney picked up the trug and began to walk down the path towards the compost heap.

She moved along the fence parallel to him. '. . . not that I see it quite that way, I suppose it's pride as much as anything. And if he thinks I'll go fifty-fifty on the house he's got another think coming. Anyway, the thing is, I'm a lot better in myself, my morale's up a lot' – she patted her hair, tweaked at her dress – 'like Judy says, I've got my life in front of me, there's no point in sitting about weeping. And Judy's going off to Marbella on a fortnight's package with Rick, that's her boyfriend, and this other bloke, and they said why not come along, bring the kid too, it'll take you out of yourself.'

Sydney emptied the trug, put it down and straightened up. He looked over the fence at the Bryans' rank and brimming garden, where all things contended and the more strident elements won: elder and couch grass and bindweed and thistles. He looked at Shirley Bryan. He said, 'You'll take the boy with you, then?'

'That's right. He'll amuse himself on the beach, he won't be

124

any trouble, and there'll always be someone to keep an eye if we want to go off to discos and that – it's a two-star hotel, it should be really nice. Rick's friend's in the car hire business, he's got this firm in north London. His marriage went bust too, Judy says.'

Sydney cleared his throat. 'If the boy's not all that keen – if he's not set on going, that is – he could stop here with me.'

Shirley stared. 'Are you sure, Mr Porter? That's ever so kind. I don't know . . . Fact is, it wouldn't be all that much fun for him, I daresay – tagging along with the four of us. I mean, I said to Judy, well, he's no trouble, he's a quiet kid, always has been, but the fact is we'd be a lot easier without him.'

Sydney said, 'Ask him what he'd like.'

'Yes. Yes. I'll do that. It's really kind. You're sure?'

'It's a question of what he'd like. The boy. It's up to him.'

*   *   *

'Thank heaven,' said Clare, 'for full-time compulsory education.'

'Have they been getting you down?'

'Oh, not really. I dote on them, as you well know. More coffee? What are you doing today?'

'Gingering up British industry. At least that will be the intention.'

'How nice it must be to live in the real world. I shall be arranging for the delivery of frock coats and agricultural smocks from a theatrical costumier.'

'Ah. The pageant. How's that going?'

'Engagingly dotty. Nevertheless, I now know more about the cost of temporarily wiring and spot-lighting the interior of a parish church than anyone in central England.'

'You must be heaven-sent, from their point of view.'

'There are those that have their doubts. Miss Bellingham would gladly see me consigned to hell – I should imagine she's been putting in a word or two in the right quarters about that already. And George Radwell is a problem.'

'I can see he would get on the nerves.'

'It's not just that. I'm afraid he has inappropriate feelings where I am concerned.'

'I beg your pardon, love?'

'He would like,' said Clare conversationally, 'to go to bed with me.'

Peter laughed, at length.

'I'm glad you take it so lightly.'

'Do you want me to have a stern word with him?'

'No, thank you. I shall manage.'

'You must admit, it's amusing.'

'Oh, hilarious. Here am I, who might be thought of as fairly privileged, and there is he.'

'A Church of England vicar,' said Peter 'though admittedly not among the affluent, would not usually be thought of as deeply deprived.'

'I wasn't talking about his income. Or mine. I was talking about being inadequate and knowing you are inadequate and failing to attract anything more vital than indifference from other people and probably knowing that too. And having presumably the normal instincts towards love and lust and other kinds of emotional participation but, apparently, neither wife nor children nor family nor friends. Nobody ever goes into the vicarage except on church business.

'I thought you didn't like him.'

'I don't think I do. That doesn't preclude guilt.'

'Guilt, with you, my girl, is a form of self-indulgence.'

'It's a good thing I'm fond of you,' said Clare, 'or I'd clock you one.'

'Why not just accept things and be thankful?'

'Some of us,' she said sweetly, 'are more complex in our responses.'

He got up. 'Well, prosaic fellow that I am, I'd better get stuck into the daily round. I hope you manage to fend off your admirers. Mind, I don't blame them, as I've often pointed out myself your . . .'

'Go away,' said Clare, 'go and get on with some industrial mismanagement.'

She sat in the empty kitchen, reading the newspaper. A ten-mile traffic jam on the M4 made the front page; elsewhere, more briefly, fire killed five children in a Nottingham terrace house, hundreds died in Indian floods.

Later, she looked out of the window at the Green and saw that the two tasteful slatted cedar litter bins had been over-turned and their contents flung around the grass. The motor-bike boys had been through again in the night. She had woken to hear them roaring past – once, twice, three times, circling the Green. She had got out of bed, infuriated, with vague notions of telephoning the police, and had seen their lights disappearing in the direction of Spelbury; the smell of high octane fuel drifted in and she closed the window. From across the landing Thomas called out and she went into his room.

'What was that noise?'

'Nothing. Some motor-bikes. Go to sleep again.'

He was barely awake. He rolled onto his side, eyes closed. 'I love you.'

'Good,' she said. 'I love you too.'

He sighed, asleep already. He had been playing with his models and lay, apparently without discomfort, in a midden of miniature bull-dozers, fire-engines, racing cars and cement mixers. She removed them and went back to bed.

Looking now at the rubbish-strewn Green, she thought about these nocturnal visitations. They seemed like the un-leashing of some elemental force, sinister and uncontrollable. It was hard to reduce them to the reality of a few restless, frustrated, destructive youths. The same people, no doubt, as handed her a pound of mince and four chops across the butcher's counter, or brushed against her in the supermarket, restocking shelves.

Presently she went out and righted the bins, cleared up the mess.

In the afternoon, when the children were back from school,

Martin Bryan came across to play with them. After a while Clare found him sitting alone on the back doorstep. He looked white.

'Are you O.K., Martin?'

'I've got a stomach ache.'

'Come and sit down inside for a bit.'

He huddled into a corner of the sofa, chewing his lip.

'Perhaps it's something you've eaten.'

He shook his head. 'I often get stomach aches. Usually they go away.'

'Does your mum know about them?'

He muttered something, his head down.

'Would you like a book to read?'

'Could I put the telly on?'

'Of course.'

He lay there, staring at the set. Clare, at the desk, wrote to her parents and dealt with some bills. When she looked across at him again she saw that he had fallen asleep, slumped across the arm of the sofa, a thin child in jeans that were too baggy for him and a T-shirt from which grinned an inane face below the caption SUNNY JIM.

* * *

'Martin's dad,' announced Thomas, 'has given him the most *fantastic* bike. It's got three speeds and a racing saddle and those bent back handle-bars. It's *fantastic*. It's bright red and it cost more than fifty pounds. His dad had it sent from the bike shop in Spelbury. Martin didn't know he was going to get it. His dad's got to go away for a long time.'

'Aren't you going to finish those sausages, Anna? Milk, Tom?'

'Three speeds. And dynamo lights.'

'That is not,' said Clare, 'a fantastic bike. A fantastic bike would have wings and be able to talk. Kindly treat the language with respect.'

'Fairy stories,' said Anna smugly, 'are fantastic.'

128

Thomas glared. 'Copy-cat. That's what Mum said, you don't know it by yourself. Copy-cat, dirty rat!'

'Shut up.'

'This bike, this *fantastic* bike, has dynamo lights and special clips at the back for a carrier.'

'Fantastic is things that aren't real, like fairy stories. So ha ha!'

'Hush,' said Clare. 'both of you. Turn your minds to something else, such as pudding, for which there is a choice of ice-cream or stewed apricots, or conceivably both.'

And she goes to the fridge, thinking with grief of Martin, who has a shiny new bike with three speeds and a racing saddle, and, with love and indulgence, of Thomas, who has a rusty old three-wheeler and does not know his own good fortune.

*   *   *

George. Not Mr Radwell. George. They had stood there in the church, chatting about this and that, he holding the end of a tape-measure for her, and she had called him George. 'George,' she had said, 'of course I quite see your point, George.' He had told her, face to face, no mincing words, what he felt about her way of looking at things, and she'd said well, of course, George, but I see it like this . . . They'd had an interesting discussion, on a different level from the sort of thing he usually met up with. She'd been wearing a blue skirt and a sort of red shirt that pulled out when she reached up to measure something, leaving this slice of bare skin, bare soft skin. He would only have had to put a hand out and he could have touched it.

'Weston-super-Mare. Or Bournemouth.'

He jumped.

Mrs Tanner stood over him, thrusting a cup of tea. 'I was saying we're reckoning on a holiday this year, seeing as I'm so much better. You're not quite with me this morning, are you, Vicar? I've sugared it for you.'

'There's sea,' said George savagely, 'at Weston-super-Mare and Bournemouth.'

129

Mrs Tanner looked at him with dignity. 'They think at the clinic I'm doing so nicely I can probably take it. It'll be a challenge, the doctor says. It's tackling things little by little, that's the secret. Made any plans for your holidays yet, Vicar?'

George muttered that he'd probably go up to Scarborough for a week or so to see his mother.

'Yes,' said Mrs Tanner. 'Well that's quite pleasant I should imagine if you've nothing special arranged. I'll get going on the kitchen, then.'

He would, as for the last five years, since Frank Brimlow with whom he was at college had married a fifty year old widow and ceased to be available for walking tours of the Lakes, spend a week in Scarborough and a weekend in Leeds. In Scarborough he would shuffle the length of the front with his mother, watch the Test on television, and put new washers on her taps. In Leeds he would stay two nights with his other college friend, in a house rowdy with children, and wonder if his visits were indeed as welcome as they were made out to be.

Last year, his mother had been in hospital at the time of his visit. Gastric trouble. He went to see her daily, walking the length of the ward to the bed at the end in which she sat, wearing a salmon-coloured nightdress. He found these walks excruciating, past the rows of swivelling eyes, the coveys of pretty, busy, confident nurses, the patients from whom sprouted disconcerting arrangements of tubes and coloured plastic bags, at which he carefully did not look. His mother would inspect his daily offerings of grapes or flowers, and take up the theme of complaint, criticism and erosion of any signs of complacency. 'That's a nice bunch of grapes. I wonder there aren't peaches in the shops yet. You'd do well to keep out of the sun, with your skin, I can see you've been out too long, you're shining like a beacon. It was the same when you were a child – no good letting you play hours on the beach like all the others, red and raw you'd be, and I'd be up all night with the calamine lotion.' Lowering her voice a little, she would embark on a run down of her neighbours by social status and medical

130

condition. 'The one in the next bed's got a husband who's a racing driver. You meet all kinds, in hospital, it's interesting, I'll say that. I've not had an interesting life, your father was a stay-at-home sort of man, not ambitious either, he could have made more of himself, but he wouldn't set about it. And then with just the one child, and you were a quiet sort of boy, you kept yourself to yourself a lot. I've not been extended. And with no grandchildren to take me out of myself.'

George would sit, mainly silent. Visiting hours two thirty to four.

'The chaplain's very nice. He's a real live wire. He has the nurses in fits sometimes. He's young, of course, nice-looking fellow.'

Dear Mother, he wrote, unfortunately I shan't be able to fit in my visit to you this summer. My new next-door neighbours, some people called Paling – I don't know if I mentioned them, he's an executive with United Electronics and she is an intelligent sort of woman, turning out a valuable helping hand over church matters – anyway, they've asked me to come along with them for a fortnight or so to this cottage they have in Wales. Peter may have to go off for a while on business and I daresay he feels he'd like to have someone around as company for Clare and the children. So, as I say, I'm afraid . . .

Dear Mother, I will be up on Friday 27th as planned, arriving Scarborough on the two-thirty train.

*   *   *

Martin sat in the place at the end of the garden, his old hiding-place in the bushes from when he was young, and thought about it. Thought about what she'd said. Did he want to or didn't he? Did he want to go to Spain with her and Auntie Judy and some other people, or didn't he? Mr Porter had said he could stay here with him if he liked.

There would be a beach in Spain, and a swimming-pool. Spain was abroad. You'd go in an aeroplane. Auntie Judy would be there. He didn't really like Auntie Judy very much:

131

she giggled a lot and whispered things to Mum and she smelt of scent all the time. And Dad wasn't going to come, Mum said. When Martin had said, 'Why? Why isn't he coming?' she'd said sharply, 'Maybe we don't want him.' So he wasn't coming but these other people were.

If he stayed here he could sleep in Mr Porter's spare room and it would be all right. Mr Porter didn't bother you, he just got on with things, but he knew good card tricks and he liked playing Halma and Attack. And he cooked good dinners, better than Mum actually; he'd stand at the stove with everything arranged round him just so, the fat and the salt and milk, frowning a bit and tutting if things weren't going right.

He wanted to be with Mum, and yet at the same time he didn't. It made him feel funny, the way she was nowadays, the things she said; he was getting his stomach aches again.

He thought he'd say he didn't want to go to Spain. He'd stay here and play cards with Mr Porter and go over to Tom's house and ride the new bike round the Green. He'd got the new bike, anyway. The red bike. The bike Dad sent.

Chapter Eleven

'You're mincing,' said the lady from the drama group. She sprang athletically from her perch on the back of a pew and advanced on Ray Turnbull, the hairdresser, black-sideboarded and tight-waistcoated as the Georgian squire. 'You're behaving as though you were in drag. Give him a bit of *machismo*.' She strode down the nave, miming the virility of status. The Swing rioters slouched on the chancel steps.

Miss Bellingham, in Puritan costume, voiced misgivings from the back of the church. 'In York they used to do these mystery plays for the Festival. All very charming and medieval. I suggested something along those lines for us but of course no one else would hear of it.'

'In the Middle Ages,' said Clare, 'they boiled people in oil. They also dropped them off castles, impaled them and flayed them alive. It wasn't universally charming.'

Miss Bellingham, smoothing the crisp white terylene of a cuff, remarked that some people had a passion for looking on the gloomy side of things.

It was hot. Outside, the Green baked in torpid sunshine, the trees sagging in the still air, the tarmac sticky underfoot. Even the church had lost its stony coolness and felt clammy; its smell was different, too – no longer that universal church aroma of brass polish, damp hymnals and dusty hassocks but a more pungent human smell of sweat and hair lacquer.

Sydney Porter, coming in, was taken aback. Until this moment, the first costume rehearsal on the spot, with lighting and so forth, he hadn't quite reckoned what it would be like. He was reminded of concert parties at Portsmouth in the war: people in the Mess done up in fancy dress for a song and dance routine. He joined Mrs Paling, standing by a pillar at the door, and watched Ray Turnbull stride up the nave once more and confront the rioters, strung out now behind the altar rail in attitudes of belligerence. He said, doubtfully, 'You can't help wondering if it's anything like it was – I mean, the actual time.'

'Quite. Never mind. That's not the point, really.'

Ray Turnbull muffed a line and there was general laughter. Sydney looked away and muttered something.

'Sorry?'

'I said you can't help feeling a bit it's not quite right, this sort of thing. Not respectful. After all it actually happened to those blokes, them that were shot, the ones that were sent to Tasmania.'

'That's the awful thing about the past. It's true.'

'You think,' Sydney went on after a moment, 'about how it might have been you or me.'

'Exactly.' They watched, together, as Ray Turnbull harangued the rioters. 'Hold it,' said the lady from the drama group, 'I'm not happy about the grouping. Can you shift left a bit, darling?'

'But the thing is,' Clare continued, 'that it's not much more of a manipulation or distortion than lots of other things. The past is always our own projection – in a sense it's quite unreal anyway.'

Sydney grunted, non-committal.

'Up to a point, we always invent it. I mean, the real past is no longer accessible, because you can never divest it of our own wisdoms and misconceptions. Like Miss Bellingham probably has Marks and Spencers knickers on under her costume, and Ray Turnbull's forgotten to take his digital watch off.'

Sydney shuffled awkwardly. He didn't know about Miss

134

Bellingham's knickers, nor want to, and Mrs Paling was getting a bit involved for his taste. 'Well,' he said, 'I'd better have a word with Mr Radwell. This stuff should be through from the printers for the programmes.' He moved away and stood waiting for the vicar to finish talking to one of the electricians, a boy in jeans and a purple T-shirt who squatted on the floor, unreeling flex and whistling through his teeth.

Sunshine, streaking slantwise through the clerestory windows, fell like spotlighting on the Doom wall-painting so that Sydney saw its details more sharply than perhaps ever before: the grey spectral figures, the spry grinning red devils. He didn't believe in hell himself, nor heaven either, not put like that. But, looking at the painting, he heard again the whine of bombs in Portsmouth harbour, the rattle of gunfire at sea, saw the smoking shell of Mansell Road. Beneath the crossing arch, Ray Turnbull and the Swing rioters played out their charade. Sydney wondered if this pageant had been all that good an idea after all. Well, they were into it now, and if it brought in the money, there was no harm done.

George could only follow one word in three of what the electrician said. Technicalities were compounded with colloquialisms. 'The thing is,' said George, 'we'd rather not have all these wires showing above the pulpit.' The boy nodded, intent on something else. 'O.K., squire, not to worry.'

The church, draped in flex, resembled the wings of a stage; spotlights clustered like exotic fruit around the capitals and at the apex of windows. From time to time, as they were tested, one section or another of the building would leap into brilliant relief, even amid the hazy sunshine; pulpit, font, altar or doorway. The whole place, George realized, had been skillfully transformed; it had become a setting, the backdrop for events. Uneasily, he wandered into the nave, noticing the changed smell and the unfamiliar noises; were it not that this kind of thing was a commonplace nowadays, and well thought of, he would have had qualms about the wisdom of it all. At St Mary's Spelbury they had concerts every first Saturday of the month, and St Damian's at Tamerton had been given over for a fortnight last summer to that art exhibition for the festival: orange and scarlet plastic sculptures all down the aisle and the chancel hung with pictures made of raffia and bits of cut-up clothing. He stood staring at the lady from the drama group, who wore a long flowery skirt and what seemed to George to be the top half of a bathing costume. Beside him, Sydney Porter was saying something about programmes.

*　　*　　*

The children, Thomas, Anna and Martin, squatted behind the big stone tomb at the end of the churchyard and argued, half-heartedly, about what to do next.

Thomas said, 'We could watch them playing dressing-up in the church'.

'It's not playing, you stupid. It's acting. They're acting real things that happened.'

Thomas, rolling on his back, sucked a grass stem. 'Stupid yourself. That's a play. A thing people act is a play. So they're playing. So ha ha.'

'I'm thirsty,' said Anna.

'So am I thirsty.'

'We could go back to the house and get iced drinks from the fridge. She's in the church with the others, I saw her go in.'

'We could have a go on Martin's bike.'

'Can I have first go on your bike, Martin?'

And Martin, a person of subtly enhanced status, exercises carefully and fairly his powers of patronage. Presently, in the endless sultry evening, the children speed round and round the Green, in turn, on the red bike with a racing saddle and dynamo lights, while, within the church, their elders simulate emotion and involvement and tempers grow short.

*　　*　　*

Sydney had drawn up a menu for the fortnight. He would know where he was then, with the shopping, and the boy

136

would get things in the right order, not too much of anything, a bit of fish for mid-week, a small roast at the weekend, stews and the odd fry-up in between. The menu, in Sydney's neat script, hung above the kitchen dresser: 'Tuesday dinner – chops & veg. Tea – ham & salad, treacle tart'. Against this, in a childish hand, was pencilled 'Chips too?'. Sydney grinned, unloading groceries. There was an unfamiliar sound in the house; it was a moment or two before he realized it was himself humming. It was a beautiful day, sun pouring into the room, the world outside a pleasure to behold, bright and fresh and clean.

*　　*　　*

It was going to be too hot again. George, getting up with a headache, looked out onto the Green and saw the trees standing already in pools of shade and heat-haze shimmering above the road. The headache was the product of a restless night, which had in turn arisen from the rehearsal, continuing too late and with gathering acrimony. The younger members of the cast, the various extras and helpers, had got bored and started larking about. The lady from the drama group fell out with Ray Turnbull and others, pitching standards over and beyond what was thought appropriate. 'It's not bloody Stratford, you know,' someone said, not *sotto voce* enough. The lady from the drama group threatened resignation; John Coggan and Harry Taylor succeeded in persuading her not to. Mrs Paling, throughout, leaned against a pillar at the back of the church, looking amused.

And then there was the business of the execution scene. The three Levellers, having been sentenced at a kangaroo court presided over by the Cromwellian colonel and taking place actually within the church, were to be dragged out into the churchyard from whence were to be heard, after a telling pause, three musket shots. 'Super,' said the lady from the drama group, who was now Iris to everybody. 'Lovely. I'll buy that. But the lead up won't do. Much much too static.' She

137

paced round the chancel, her face contorted in thought, moving people from place to place. 'Stand there a minute, love, let's see what that looks like.' Presently she announced, 'I've got it! We have the colonel's wife throw herself on one of the prisoners and try to hold him back by force. Right? He's been her lover, that's the thing – that's why she's so mad keen to get them off, it all comes out when she realizes they're actually going to be shot.'

'It didn't happen,' said Sydney Porter stolidly.

'All right. So it didn't. But it might have done.'

'That's a point,' said Harry Taylor. 'I mean, how's anyone to know what happened and what didn't?'

'Oh, go on!' cried the barmaid from the Crossed Keys, 'let's put it in! Who'm I going to throw meself at, then? Jim?'

Sydney Porter, having repeated again that it never happened, removed himself to the back of the church in disassociation. There was argument. Iris stalked off to sit on the altar steps. 'No way do I rehearse that scene again like it was. It's dull dull dull.'

And George had found himself butting in. He didn't like Iris and he didn't, suddenly, like what had happened to the church and he didn't like all this to-ing and fro-ing about something which, if it had been thus, then could not have been otherwise. As someone who all his life had hoped that what palpably was might somehow turn out to be quite other, he knew all about that. You do not through force of fantasy acquire personal magnetism or qualities of leadership or sexual success. You are stuck with the way things are. Or were. He said, 'Bit pointless, really, if this woman wasn't really there anyway. I mean, the thing is, we were trying to have scenes from the church's past. This wouldn't be, would it – what you're suggesting?'

'Oh, for goodness' sake!' Iris snapped. 'Do you people have to be so frightfully realistic? I mean, do you want this show to be a success or not?'

George felt himself redden; he heard his voice grow shriller; he heard his snorty laugh. He saw contempt in Iris's eyes;

138

he saw the exasperated lift of her eyebrows. And who, she implied, are you? He felt his supporters fall away. 'Oh, come on, Vicar,' someone said, 'she's got a point. I mean, it does drag a bit. Fine once they're onto the execution.' 'Oh, *Vicar*,' said Iris. 'Terribly sorry, I didn't realize. But look, now don't you see . . .'

And all of a sudden Clare Paling had been there, arrived from nowhere, stepping cool and calm from shadows, proposing this and that. Iris switched her attention, alert to a superior presence. 'Quite,' said George. 'That's just what I was going to suggest.' But no one was listening to him any more. 'O.K.,' Iris was saying. 'O.K., I like it, let's try it out. Mandy throws himself on her husband, not the prisoner, he wasn't her lover, she's just a soft-hearted lady. Mandy, love, let's have a run through of that . . .'

And, in the soupy evening heat and gloom, moths banging against the spotlights, they got down to it yet again. It was eleven o'clock before George locked the church and went home to bed.

*   *   *

'We're fine,' said Clare to Brussels. 'A bit hot, if anything. Mistral weather. Bad temper weather. They had the rehearsal last night, with lighting and everyone in full fig. What? Oh, all right, except that they were ganging up on the vicar, poor wretch.'

And that, for reasons she was unable exactly to define, would not do. Sympathy for the under-dog? Unwillingness to see anyone trounced by that harpy in the eastern get-up? Sheer meddling? Whichever it may have been, there had come a point when she could no longer loiter in the shelter of the nave, idly watching; when, suddenly, the spectacle of George Radwell making things worse for himself with every blundering remark had become intolerable. Persecution will not do, even of those who invite it.

'Sorry? No, love, I am not harbouring a secret passion,

139

merely a bit of everyday charity. Or maybe local patriotism is breaking out. It's neither here nor there. When shall we see you?'

He had lurked around in the aisle, George, fidgeting, tripping over a cable once and fetching up on his knees so the actors were giggling behind their hands. And then he had stumbled into an argument with Iris – she sitting on the altar steps with her chin cupped in her hands and eyebrows raised at this red-faced quacking fool. And the more he bleated on the more irritated became the onlookers, the cooler and the more destructive Iris's rejoinders. On the pulpit steps, out of George's range of vision, someone was imitating his mannerisms. And it would not do, Clare found. Despite the fact, she uncomfortably thought, that that is much as I have behaved to him too, in my time.

She put the receiver down. The copper beech on the Green, sun shining through its leaves, was a glowing port wine red, incandescent, shimmering; a butterfly, opening and closing its wings in the warmth of the windowsill, was finely dusted with golden fur; Thomas, speeding past on Martin Bryan's bike, thin brown legs stretched to the utmost to reach the pedals, fair head bent low over the handlebars, was charged with the wild grace and energy of a young animal: a kitten, a puppy. When the world looks as it does, she thought, how can it be that there is anything wrong with it?

*   *   *

Martin said, 'I'm four hundred and twenty seven and you're five hundred and six.'

The rummy score, accumulating every evening, two neat columns, was on a pad propped on the mantelpiece. Alongside it was the Attack! score (straight wins and losses) and the Halma score. They were thinking of switching from Halma to Draughts.

'There was a postcard from Mum in the house.'

'Ah,' said Sydney.

'She said it's ever so hot and she's got a smashing tan. Are we having cocoa or Ovaltine?'

They considered.

'Ovaltine,' said Martin. 'It was cocoa last night. Shall I put the chocolate digestives on the tray?'

'No harm.'

It was almost dark, the windows open to the sultry night. Continuing warm and dry, the weather forecast had said, possibility of thundery showers in the south. Sydney drew the curtain and sat down, picking up his cup. 'Have to get the hose out tomorrow.'

They drank. 'Tell me about the time you were in that action off the Persian Gulf.'

'We had that last night.'

'Actually I'd like it again.' said Martin.

And Sydney, who is not a man given to reminiscence, tells again. And with the telling there comes a curious cleansing of the head. The sounds are still there, and the sights, but they slip somehow into another dimension: they have lost resonance. He reaches the end of the account, and pauses. 'There's a naval hat-band upstairs I've kept. *HMS Reliant*. Souvenir. You could have it, I daresay.'

Martin's eyes widen. 'Could I?'

Sydney finishes his drink, stacks the cups on the tray.

'It 'ud have been for Jennifer, but of course she was gone by then.'

'Jennifer?' says Martin.

*   *   *

George, coming into one of the several empty bedrooms in the vicarage in search of an active light-bulb, caught sight of himself in the freckled wardrobe mirror. The wardrobe, empty, was the only piece of furniture in the room except for an iron bedstead and a couple of chairs. It had been given him by a parishioner who had no use for it and acquired in the giving a pleasing glow of charity. Much of George's furniture had come to him in this way; the sofa downstairs, the sofa of the broken spring, had been Miss Bellingham's until she replaced it with a new, chintz-covered suite. He saw himself in the oval, brownish mirror, advancing through murky sunshine in which spun columns of dust: a man with thickening waist and thinning sandy hair, rather older than George had thought. The man sat down on the bed and continued to look at himself in the mirror.

Some while ago, ten years or so, it had come to George – in the middle of Evensong, in fact – that he had lost what faith he had. When he was young, fresh from college, he had believed, or believed that he believed; more importantly, he had been shored up by membership of an institution. He was no longer on his own; he was a part of something large and solid. All that had come, over the years, to seem less sustaining. And now, stumbling through the Magnificat with Miss Bellingham, Sydney Porter, and seven other members of the congregation, he realized that he felt nothing at all; that he had not prayed, in months, with any expectation of comfort. He stared over the top of Miss Bellingham's head at the rose window and tried to assess what he felt about this: there should be an aching void, but there was not. He did not feel particularly easy, but neither did he feel particularly bereft. Over the next days and weeks he thought the matter over. Should he discuss things with those who were available for such purposes? Should he leave the Church? He shrank from both courses. And in the end he decided, if decision it could be called, that he both could and would perform his duties as adequately or inadequately as he ever had, that while not easy in his mind he was not a great deal less easy than he ever had been, and that he might as well go on as he was.

The man in the mirror wore grey flannel trousers baggy at the knees, blue open-necked shirt and corduroy jacket with a rip in the sleeve. He had a pink shiny face whose features seemed to George an unfair travesty of the studio portrait on his mother's mantelpiece in Scarborough: the carefully cosmetic

142

photograph of a fresh-faced reliable-looking young man in clerical dress. He looked at the man and the man looked relentlessly back.

He had made a fool of himself at the rehearsal last night. He had bumbled into an argument with that woman Iris and she had made mincemeat of him. He had seen, out of the corner of one eye, mocking faces; he had known that those who might have agreed with what he said were growing impatient and hostile. He had not known how to extricate himself. And then Mrs Paling had stepped in and put an end to it. Afterwards, he had wanted to say something to her – not a further humiliation by thanks, but some acknowledgement. Looking round, though, as the church emptied, he found her already gone: across the Green, he had seen her lit and curtained bedroom window.

George, and the man in the mirror, continued to sit in the empty room, in silent mutual observation. The rectangle of sunlight on the floor changed planes and began to climb the side of the wardrobe. A fly that had been patrolling the windowsill walked into a spider's web and died with flailing wings. Bring me a woman like Mrs Paling, said George. Please. God. Before it is much too late. Make me a person able to cope with a woman like Mrs Paling.

He removed the light-bulb from the ceiling fitting and went downstairs.

Chapter Twelve

Anna sits with eyes clenched shut and an expression of religious fervour.

'Anna! I said, more cream?'

'Ssh! I'm wishing. I've got a wish because I took the last strawberry.'

'Huh!' says Thomas. 'I could have had the last strawberry if I wanted. Anyway, wishes don't come true. What are you wishing?'

'Not telling you.'

'I know anyway.'

'Don't be stupid. How can you? He doesn't, does he, Mum?'

'Yes I do. You're wishing for a Cindy doll and bikini like Julie Stevens and a calculator.'

'Shut up!' bawls Anna, scarlet and tearful. 'Shut up! It spoils it if you say?'

'When *I* wish,' says Thomas smugly, 'I don't wish *things*. I wish for there to be no more thunderstorms or earthquakes ever and for people not to die any more. I wish for everyone to be happy for ever and ever.'

'That's *stupid*!' Anna snaps, 'because it couldn't happen. Could it, Mum?'

Clare looks thoughtfully at her daughter. 'You've got a point there. Whereas a Cindy doll and a bikini . . .'

'Ssh!' wails Anna. 'Don't *say* . . .'

'What do you wish for, Mum,' says Thomas, 'when you wish?'

Clare gets up from the table. 'That would be telling.'

When I was your age and beyond, I went into churches to do my wishing. Having given that up, I suppose I have given up wishing too. Besides, for people like me, a wish is something negative: my requests would be to avert the hand of fate, not to be granted further indulgences. I have had more than my fair share already, it always seems to me. But then, nothing is fair; we know that.

She piles crockery into the sink, watching Anna and Thomas rush jostling one another down the garden path: Thomas, who still has the faith to wish for the world to be different; Anna, who has learned to settle for a Cindy doll. Is that, Clare wonders, what is meant by loss of innocence?

And presently she goes upstairs to Anna's bedroom which is, as it happens, a pair to the empty bedroom in the vicarage, in which George Radwell is at this moment staring at his reflection in a mottled mirror. The two houses, built 1905, are a similar design. There, though, the likeness ends. Anna's bedroom is prettily wallpapered with a willow leaf pattern and the bed has a patchwork cover; there are bright cotton rugs on the polished floor and curtains that match the wallpaper. There is a pine dressing-table with brass handles, laden with a clutter of Anna's things: hairbrush and one dirty sock and a green glass cat with broken tail and a postcard collection in a shoebox and a packet of Smarties (empty). Clare picks up the sock and looks at herself in Anna's bamboo-framed mirror. She sees a woman with a long thin face and straight hair, lately streaked by the sun: a woman with, it seems to her, a somewhat uncompromising stare, probably offputting. The mouth is wide, of the kind meaninglessly known as a generous mouth. Generous in what way? I am not particularly generous, Clare thinks. What have I ever done for anyone, except for my nearest and dearest, which does not count.

She observes herself with a certain cynicism: a woman of

thirty-five, handsome in her way, charged with undirected energy, a fatalist and insufficiently charitable. In another age, she thinks, there would have been a vocation for a woman like me; I could have been a saint, or a prostitute.

* * *

The banner, reaching almost the length of the churchyard wall, was slung from a lamp-post to the branch of the big yew. It said 'Church of St Peter and St Paul, Laddenham: Ninth Centenary'. At the lych-gate was a poster on a board, giving the times of the three performances of the pageant. The apparatus for flood-lighting the church was mounted on one of the telephone poles at the side of the Green. These three unfamiliar arrangements contrived to give the whole Green an air of carnival: everything was subtly changed. Attention was focused on the church so that instead of squatting apologetic-ally behind the churchyard wall it appeared to have grown; the Amoco Garage, in turn, seemed smaller and shabbier.

In the evening, the evening before the first performance, when the flood-lighting was switched on for the first time, this effect became even more pronounced. Around the Green, the houses glimmered. The garage harshly shone. But the church was suspended golden in the night, a faery creation not of stone but the very stuff of dreams, detached from time and place, fabulous. The children, intoxicated with the unreality of it all, wheeled about the Green shrieking and yelling in the darkness. Anna, dashing into the house, cried 'Come and see, Mum! You must come and see. It's *beautiful*! It's the most beautiful thing I ever saw. It's as beautiful as the stage when we went to the ballet.'

Sydney, standing at his kitchen window, was reminded of the lights coming on in Piccadilly after the war. The cheering, the faces up-turned to rippling red and green and gold electric bulbs. Then, too, a known landscape was transfigured, trans-mogrified. He looked now at St Peter and St Paul and saw it hang in the night like a ship against the black globe of the sea.

he saw the children capering under the chestnuts on the Green and wondered about calling the boy in: it was gone half past nine. But then he saw Mrs Paling come out of her garden gate and walk purposefully across the road, returning after a minute with two small dancing figures behind her. Moments later he heard his own front door open, and put a pan of milk on the stove.

From the window of George's study, the church appeared to be trapped in a great shaft of light, indeed to be, perhaps, itself some reflective trick of the light: a mirage. He found the effect both compelling and disturbing and sat for a long while at his desk unable to take his eyes off it, not knowing if he found it vulgar or ethereal. He was reminded of garish souvenirs at Catholic shrines: postcards of St Bernadette in her rock, lit up like a Christmas tree. And at the same time there came the memory of fascinating childhood story books in which magic, glowing castles beckoned from misty landscapes, mysterious with promise.

'Isn't it beautiful!' cried Anna, turning at the door for a last look. 'I wish it was always like that.'

And Clare, standing for a moment before closing the door, saw a building bathed in fiery light, lacking only a Blakean God to point an awful finger at them all.

*   *   *

At midnight George, who is operating a rota system with Sydney Porter and John Coggan, turns off the switch. The apparition vanishes and the Green settles down to sleep.

The church, dark and empty in the small hours, is poised for action. Cables hang like torpid serpents or are tucked under pews; the spotlights, precisely adjusted, stare blindly down at the altar, at the pulpit, at the point in the nave from which the Cromwellian soldiers will drag the renegades out into the churchyard to their death. In the vestry, the men's costumes are hung where George's surplice and the choir's gear would normally be: these have been temporarily put away. The

147

women are to dress in the vicarage and make their way as unobtrusively as possible across the Green and in by the west door. There is a row of muskets propped against the hymn book cupboard and a top hat slung jauntily above a stack of nineteenth century agricultural smocks: the muskets, of course, are mock-ups and the smocks made of a lightweight synthetic fibre guaranteed to minimize discomfort. The real thing would be heavy and constricting.

In the nave, the thirteenth century foliate mask, which has seen a thing or two in its time, gazes stonily at the stereo and loudspeakers which will provide the music. The church is silent now, except for those creakings and saggings peculiar to an old building, as to an old body.

Presently, at about one-thirty, these stirrings are enlarged by other sounds: there is tinkle of breaking glass and the click of a window latch being opened.

*　　*　　*

Sydney was in the nave, heading for the vestry, before he realized anything was wrong. There'd been nothing in the porch to tell you, nothing at all. He'd unlocked the door as usual, looking for nothing because expecting nothing, walked past the font and the central pews, turned to go towards the vestry, and stopped because there was wet under his feet; wet, and something else – brown, sticky. And then he looked up and saw.

Saw the aerosol paint on the pillars and all over the capitals and the foliate mask and the font. SHIT and WANKERS and things he couldn't read that trailed off into loops and blots. Saw the screen and the altar rails pitted with cigarette burns like old-fashioned poker work. Saw the broken glass on the altar; the east window starred and cracked. Saw now what was on the floor. Saw the slashed hassocks spewing stuffing everywhere and the heaps of shredded hymn books and the smashed spotlights and the cables ripped from their fittings.

And then he smelled scorching. He went into the vestry

148

and saw the pile of costumes on the floor, ripped and paint-spattered and faintly smoking. He saw the systematically broken muskets and the top hat trampled to fragments. He stepped through glass to close the window. He filled the big brass flower jug with water and poured it onto the smouldering heap of garments, turned them with his foot and poured on another jugfull. They'd made a bad job of that, the sods; it took a right charlie not even to be able to start a fire properly.

Then he went out into the churchyard and wiped his shoes on the grass, to and fro, to and fro. He was shaking all over, he realized.

*   *   *

Clare looked first for the Doom painting. No one had said anything about that. She wandered through the debris, the glass and the mangled hassocks and the leaves from hymn books, and stared up at the crossing arch. Not touched, thank heaven. Heaven? Well, thank whatever or whoever is appropriate. Intact for another few hundred years, let us hope. Why didn't they have a go at it? Too high? Too dingy? Well, thanks be anyway.

She had stopped in the churchyard to talk to a policeman investigating the long grass at the foot of the wall.

'Will you catch them?'

'Hard to say. We'll do our damnedest, but . . .' the man shrugged '. . . they don't leave you much to go on. Could be from Spelbury; could not be.'

'Why on earth did none of us hear anything?'

'Because they left the bikes round in Pound Lane or some-where like that, came over the wall, broke the vestry window and in that way. Once inside – well, there'd have been a fair bit of racket but I daresay it wouldn't carry outside that much.'

'They've been here before, I suppose people have told you that?'

The policeman nodded. 'If it's the same lot.'

'It's appalling,' said Clare. 'It never occurred to any of

us . . . I suppose we should have had someone guarding the place.'

The man prodded the grass, retrieved a cigarette package, put it in a plastic bag. 'In the end, you're a bit helpless with this kind of thing. It's like fate, there's not too bloody much you can do about it.'

Harry Taylor, John Coggan and George were moving about the shattered church, gingerly, shell-shocked, it seemed. Sydney Porter was swabbing down the floor with mop and bucket. Miss Bellingham, brisk and businesslike as some relief worker in the wake of calamity, was gathering litter into a pile. She said to Clare, 'Ah, there you are, Mrs Paling. Well, I suppose one could have seen this coming, in this day and age. I'm wondering if we couldn't salvage a few of these hymnals, if one of us got down to it with some sellotape.'

The men were talking in hushed voices – a curious contrast to the stridencies of yesterday's rehearsal. Harry Taylor said, 'I suppose conceivably if we all worked like blacks all day . . . And if the costumiers could . . .'

'They can't,' said Clare, 'I've already rung them. Not a hope.'

'Then that's that, I suppose.'

'We shall have to refund people who've already bought tickets.'

They stared at the paint-daubed pillars. Clare thought of medieval churches, ablaze with colour. John Coggan said, 'It strikes me now, too late in the day, that there would have been insurance cover . . .'

'The policies are all up to date,' George interrupted. 'I checked right away. The people we've always dealt with are . . .'

'I didn't mean the church's insurance. I meant insurance against cancellation of the pageant.'

'Ah. Well, of course that seemed such an outside contingency.'

'Nothing,' said Clare bitterly, 'is an outside contingency.'

They were united in outrage, all incompatibilities shelved. Miss Bellingham came up. 'Cup of tea. I filled a thermos as soon as I heard, to bring over. I thought, it's going to be all hands to the wheel, we shall need this. My sister and I did volunteer work at one of the London evacuation centres. Of course, none of you people are old enough to remember the war.'

George Radwell walked away into the chancel. After a moment Clare followed him, a steaming plastic mug in her hand. He seemed a man deflated; he had stood in silence through much of the discussion about what had immediately to be done. Now, he was staring at the glass-strewn altar. The embroidered cover had been efficiently and systematically ripped with a knife; the wooden candlesticks lay on the floor, snapped in half.

Clare said, 'How very Cromwellian.'

'Mmn.'

'It's hard to understand if this kind of thing is deliberate venom, or just pure mindlessness.'

He had been thinking of Stoke Newington, where once disaffected members of the Youth Club had scrawled graffiti on tombstones and robbed the offertory box. You thought you were immune from that sort of thing in Laddenham. In Stoke Newington, the vicar had traced the culprits and talked earnestly to them for hours; a boyish, enthusiastic chap he'd been, a keen football supporter. His wife was a dark wiry girl who'd seen all the latest films and gave spaghetti suppers in the vicarage. 'Do come, George' she used to say, always as an afterthought. 'The more the merrier.' She had the same long sinewy legs as Clare Paling. Mrs Paling's legs, today, were shrouded in white cotton trousers. She was talking now about the aerosol paint on the stonework and the need for specialist advice on its removal. She handed him a mug of tea and he looked through the spiralling steam at the smashed window and noted that she had sought him out, that she had come deliberately to talk to him, that her voice had a different tone.

The tone of pity, he thought. She is sorry for me. He stood there drinking the tea in the midst of destruction and it struck him that never before had he known the church so filled with goodwill. Not at Christmas nor weddings nor christenings. Did it take so much to create that? Did you have to smash stained glass windows and abuse ancient stone to make people well disposed towards one another? He looked at Mrs Paling, who was examining the candlesticks and asking to take them home to mend with some miraculous new glue; she had a flowered shirt above the white trousers and her face was screwed up in concentration as she tried to fit together the pieces of candlestick. Miss Bellingham and Sydney Porter were manoeuvring a sheet filled with debris out through the porch; 'Mind now, dear,' Miss Bellingham was saying, 'don't catch yourself on that nail – that's the way . . .' By the pulpit, Harry Taylor and John Coggan quietly conferred.

Clare looked up from the candlesticks at George Radwell. He is not, she thought, taking in a word I am saying. His slightly protuberant blue eyes gazed vacantly into the mug of tea; the hand that held it shook a little. She said, 'It'll be all right, you know.'

'What?'

'It'll be put right, in no time at all.' She gestured towards the window, the altar, the nave. 'It looks disastrous, but it'll be put right in no time. You see. The place is more resilient than that. It's infuriating about the pageant – the appeal – but that too, it can be made up.'

He was trying to find somewhere to put the mug. She put out her hand. 'Here, I'll give it back to Miss Bellingham.'

'Thank you.'

'I'll go and start on the vestry,' she said. 'The costumiers want to know just what the losses are, for the insurance.'

'Ah. Yes. Good.'

She hesitated. 'You're, er, all right?'

He looked at her. People were not usually solicitous about

him; certainly not people like Clare Paling. She must, he thought, be confusing him with the church itself. 'I'm all right,' he said.

*   *   *

People had got into the church in the night and spoiled all the things for the pageant and smashed windows and written rude words on the walls. Nobody was allowed in. There was a policeman at the lych-gate and only the vicar and Mr Coggan and people could go in. Thomas had got into the porch and seen through the door before someone told him to go away and he said there was fuck in big letters like on the fence by the school playground.

Mr Porter had found it. He had come back all white and angry and Martin hadn't known what to do. He stood around feeling it was his fault, like he used to feel it was his fault when he heard them arguing downstairs, Mum and Dad. He felt as though really he had done it and presently policemen would come and say, 'Martin Bryan . . .' And then Mr Porter looked up and said, 'Better get along to school, son.' Outside there were policemen, but they weren't interested in Martin; he rode past on the bike and saw them hunting about in the churchyard and he knew it was nothing to do with him and it was silly to feel it was his fault.

Mum would be back from Spain on Monday and he wouldn't stay with Mr Porter any more. He'd be going there in the evenings, though, to play Halma and Rummy, and they were thinking of making one of those model railway layouts, the ones you do yourself with plaster of paris and then you paint them. Mr Porter said he'd always rather fancied trying his hand at one of those, and there was room enough in the box room to set it out. There was a model railway set, engine and six trucks and eighteen feet of rail, in Bland's in the High Street, marked down in the sale.

He'd have liked to tell Dad about the model railway layout and how they were going to make the trees out of bits of

153

sponge painted green, but he didn't know how to write to him. There'd been another postcard from Mum but she hadn't said when he was coming back. There hadn't been any postcards from Dad; perhaps he was in a place where they didn't have interesting postcards. That was probably why.

*   *   *

The church, all day, is the centre of attention. Even those who have never set foot within its doors gather at the gate to stare and cluck; offers of help come from all sides. A man from Spelbury Town Hall who is said to know much about removing graffiti from stonework arrives and inspects. By midday, the glazier is at work. The ruined costumes are piled into the back of a van and the vestry scoured. In the afternoon, an expert from the church restoration firm turns up to have a look at the screen; he squats in front of it, eyes screwed up, contemplating its scars. The police come and go all day. They scrutinize the churchyard and fill six plastic bags with litter. One thing less, Sydney thinks drily, for me to do.

There will be a service on Sunday, as usual.

All day, Sydney, Clare, George and Miss Bellingham work. They are joined by Mrs Harrison and some ladies from the Mothers' Union; John Coggan and Harry Taylor have to go to their respective offices but will return in the evening. Miss Bellingham pops home for lunch and comes back with more thermoses and a cake baked by her sister. She spends much of the afternoon sorting mangled hymnals and recalling experiences in Deptford during the war, when she and her sister worked twelve hour shifts at the relief centre and people were so marvellous, when there was no slacking and everyone was grateful for small mercies. Her eyes shine and there are red feverish spots on each cheek; she is a little high on calamity, Clare realizes.

Clare, for her part, has dirty marks all over her white trousers and her shirt is dark with sweat. The temperature is

154

again in the seventies and she has gathered up and sorted all the slashed hassocks, some of which can be repaired by Mrs Harrison and her cronies, meticulously swept the pews of broken glass, scrubbed a part of the nave, checked and disposed of the costumes. She drinks a mug of tea with Mrs Harrison and finds that Mrs Harrison's Sharon and her Anna are deskmates at school; they agree in approval of the teacher but wish the children were doing more maths.

At four o'clock there is a flurry. The Archdeacon has come. George, shirt-sleeved at the altar, picking slivers of glass from between two boards, looks up to see the bustling dark-suited figure, hands outstretched in commiseration. 'Ah, Radwell, I came the moment my secretary . . .' They tour the church together; the Archdeacon beams upon the workers, confers with the restoration expert, has a word with the police sergeant. In the porch, they pass Clare Paling, banging dusty hassocks. The Archdeacon beams again and says it is heartening for the vicar to have such wonderful support. Clare Paling bares her teeth at him but does not reply.

And later, in the still stagnant heat of early evening, it is decided to put the flood-lighting on again tonight, for one last time. A gesture, declares Miss Bellingham. Pity not to get the benefit, says Harry Taylor, while the gear's still all in situ.

*　　　　*　　　　*

George, coming into the vicarage, was knocked out suddenly by weariness. He went into the study and sat down on the sofa without even putting the light on. His limbs ached. All day people had been asking him things and telling him and his head was a jumble of what must be done: letters, phone calls, arrangements. What he could not understand was the neutrality of his feelings. Louts had done thousands of pounds worth of damage, some of it irreparable, dished the pageant and with it for the time being the Appeal Fund, and he could feel no rage, merely a shocked resignation. They had no faces,

155

these people; what they had done was as elemental and impersonal as weather – a hurricane, a flood. You picked up the pieces.

He sat in the gathering dark and outside the floodlight went on and the church rose suddenly in the blank space of the window, a golden castle in the sky, turretted and glowing, untethered to time or place. A vision. He sat staring at it; it made him think of those banal illustrations in children's Bibles, angels appearing in a golden sunburst, incandescent Gabriels slung against a starry sky. Clare Paling smiling from the east window of the church, removing her blouse. Promises. Dreams. Today Mrs Paling had stood talking to him in the chancel, with sympathy in her eyes, and he had heard only one word in ten of what she said and he had not wanted to put out his hand and touch her arm, her thigh.

He was unbearably tired.

'Vicar? You there?'

He must have left the front door open. Mrs Tanner, monumental in the gloom, stood in the entrance. There was a smell of cooking.

'I said to my husband, I think I'll take Mr Radwell round a dish of the steak and kidney, they've been in the church since breakfast, he'll have nothing in the house. Your electric hasn't gone, has it?' She snapped the hall switch on. George stood blinking.

'That's very kind,' he said. 'I must have . . .'

'Sat there in the dark like that . . .' She marched to the kitchen. 'Ten minutes it'll want, on high, just to heat through again.' She looked at him curiously. 'There's a rip in that jacket, did you know? I'd offer to mend it but it looks too far gone to me. Well, what a day. They say there was muck, as well as the damage.'

'Yes.'

'You wouldn't believe it, would you? Well, I'll be off. My husband's walking along to meet me at the corner.'

156

He put the pie in the oven, went back into the study, into the darkness. He stood at the window. Outside, the leaves of the chestnuts and the copper beech swam in the beams of the floodlighting, multi-coloured dancing fish; the church glimmered; children swooped in the shadows, Anna and Thomas, Thomas leaping at the Bryan boy on his red bike, his red bike with the curving handles and high saddle, crying 'My turn! My go now!' And the bike hurtled off again, round the Green, into the darkness at the far side, back again into the floodlighting, past the church, past the vicarage, past Mrs Tanner stepping massive into the road.

The lorry, coming from the High Street, must have masked the solitary motor-bike behind, masked both sight and sound; the lorry, slowing to let Mrs Tanner across so that the impatient cyclist pulls out, screams ahead, swerves wildly round the trundling figure of Mrs Tanner, round her and into the bike, the red racing bike, which spins sideways onto the pavement flinging from it a rag-doll shape that goes tumbling into the wheels of the lorry.

Afterwards, he could not remember going outside. He had been there at the window with it happening in front of him and then by some unsensed propulsion he was outside on the pavement and Clare Paling was coming out of her front gate. She was saying something; not to him, not to anyone, just to the air. She was saying 'No, no, no. Please God no. Please, please, no.' The driver of the lorry was getting down from his cab and Mrs Tanner was standing on the far side of the road and someone else was running along the pavement and there was a man on a motor-bike, a middle-aged man removing his crash helmet and staring backwards.

And Anna and Thomas were standing at the edge of the Green. Anna and Thomas. Thomas and Anna.

Later, he remembered that they stood there for quite a long time. Nobody took any notice of them, after the first minute or two. George looked up and they were still there, frozen in the flood-lighting, looking no longer themselves but smaller

157

and more detached, the anonymous children at any scene of horror on a news film, in a newspaper photograph: shocked by the world. There they stood, and suddenly Anna's face turned red and ugly with tears and she ran into the house by herself, making a strange noise, neither a sob nor a scream.

Chapter Thirteen

'They're saying he didn't die quite straight away. You don't like to think about it, do you? He was alive for quite a bit after. They said he was asking for his mother in the ambulance. It was his back, see, it got him across the back. They said if he'd lived he'd have been paralysed. I saw the whole thing. I said to my sister, there I was stepping onto the pavement and I turned just in time and I saw the whole thing.'

It must be the morning, then. Somehow the night had gone, as they do, and it was the morning.

'You been on that sofa all night, Vicar?'

Presumably. And in a lot of other places too. He went through to the kitchen and put the kettle on.

'I don't mind a cup myself, if you're making a pot. It's a terrible shock, a thing like that. I've not slept well, not a bit well. My husband had to get up twice and get me an aspirin.'

He couldn't remember where the sugar was kept. He stood staring at the dresser, seeing many things, but not sugar. Wheels and Anna Paling's crumpled face and, for some reason, a part of the wall-painting in the church. Not sugar.

'Were you still out there when that Mr Porter from opposite was walking about the Green all by himself? After the ambulance had gone. Up and down, like that. You'd have thought he was gone a bit funny. Of course, it's not a nice thing to have happen, almost on your doorstep. That lady from down the road came and took him in her house, her with the two little girls. The kettle's on the boil.'

He must have fallen asleep, sometime after midnight, and then had woken again and seen the church floodlighting still on and remembered that he had undertaken to switch it off. He went across the empty Green in the tranquil night and turned the switch in the church porch, the apparition was snapped off, the castle in the sky, the golden pile. He looked into the church for a moment, quiet and silent and smelling of detergent and polish, and walked back through balmy rustling darkness.

He attended death once a week or so; had done for fifteen years. He received the coffin on the chancel steps and turned to the altar with the appropriate words. He stood at the graveside in sun or wind or rain and spoke more words. He saw people putting on a brave face; or not. He performed necessary rites; the facts of the matter, by then, did not come into it. Once a woman had said bitterly, 'Why him? Tell me that, why him?'; she had had a little boy in tow, the husband was only thirty-five, George gathered. He'd had to mumble something and turn in relief to an old mother, talking of memorials.

The facts of the matter, this time, were with him all the night; sitting in darkness on the sofa or plunging into dream-racked feverish sleep. He saw the child, the bike, Clare Paling's face livid in the flood-lighting, Anna and Thomas. He had never spoken to the other boy; for some reason this troubled him. But he never knew what to say to children.

At one point, when it was all over, he had found himself standing beside Mrs Paling on the empty pavement. She had turned and they had bleakly looked at each other for a moment and then she had gone into her own house.

*   *   *

Peter said, 'I could come back. I could get on a plane this afternoon.'

'No. Don't. Finish what you're doing. We'll see you on Friday.'

'You're sure you're all right?'

'I'm all right.'

'The children?'

'They went to school. It seemed the best thing.'

'Quite. Well, bye then, love. Take care of yourself.'

She put the phone down. It was raining. The day had begun, she had seen it begin, with a liverish yellow sky and thunder distantly rolling and now the rain had come. She had a curious sensation, stemming presumably from shock and lack of sleep, that the floors were tipping; she walked gingerly about the house, like someone old, pausing to put her hand on pieces of furniture.

She wanted Peter badly, and yet did not. The strength of his presence would perhaps have seen her through, and he would have had the sensitivity to ask no questions, but at the same time she knew she was better alone. It had taken determination to send the children to school. She had longed to keep them by her, their bodies within sight and touch; had known that they must go, that it was essential they went. She watched them trudge off into the rain, wearing plastic macks, scarlet and orange, vivid as boiled sweets.

In the middle of the morning she thought of Sydney Porter and was horrified that she had not already done so. She threw on an anorak and walked across the sodden Green. For a long time there was no answer to her knock. Then at last a bolt rattled, the door opened. He looked at her as though he had never seen her before. 'Yes?'

'I wondered – I just wondered if you were all right.'

He stared. The shuttered stare of an old man; mistrustful, parrying interference.

'If,' she said desperately, 'there's anything you need . . .'

'Nothing. Very kind.'

'A bit of company. Later, maybe. Do please, just, you know – say.'

'Company?' Bitterness, now, not mistrust. 'I'm accustomed to being on my own. Quite accustomed. Been on my own thirty-eight years.' He began to close the door.

'If you'd like me to take Martin's things,' she went on, deliberate, insisting, 'keep them till his mother . . .'

Expressionless, his old face; just the eyes flickering, at the name, suffering. 'All in hand already. Thanks all the same. Very kind.' The door closed. She turned away.

On the Green, men were dismantling the floodlighting apparatus. George Radwell came toward her. 'Sydney Porter. I remembered of course the boy had been staying with him. But you've already been. Is he all right?'

'I don't think so,' said Clare, 'but there isn't anything he'll let anyone do.'

George nodded. He looked, she thought, knocked out, drained. He nodded again, barely glancing at her, and turned to go to the church. It came to her as extraordinary that they had moved together, she and this man, through the previous day; like being trapped with a stranger in a lift. But he was not, now, a stranger. We are in the world with other people, she thought, like it or not. I don't dislike George Radwell any more; now why is that? She said, with diffidence, so that he looked at her in perplexity as though perhaps he had not quite heard, 'I've got this stew we never got around to last night – come and help me eat it now if you're not too busy.'

*   *   *

He sat on a sofa in a room that mirrored the vicarage study in dimensions and outlook. In every other way it was so unlike as to induce a sense of cultural shock: there were bare polished boards instead of worn carpeting and many pictures and books rampant in the alcoves beside the fireplace. The sofa was covered in some striped material and had no broken spring. The room smelt of flowers, not damp: there was a bowl of branches from some flowering bush on the table.

Clare Paling squatted at a cupboard. 'Sherry? Martini? Or vodka if you like the stuff, or whisky or Pernod or God knows what. You name it, we have it. Duty free, of course. Peter goes to Brussels every other week, I think I'm going to have a gin, which is not normal for me at this time of day but I feel pretty awful.'

He said, 'The children . . .?'

'They're as all right as can be expected. They didn't go to sleep for a long time.'

She went to the kitchen. He sat looking at a picture above the mantelpiece, a bright, rather childish painting of red and blue flowers in a pot; he supposed the childish quality to be deliberate, an inverted sophistry. He didn't know anything about pictures.

Dear mother, Yesterday vandals smashed up the church and a child was killed by a lorry outside the vicarage door. I have been lunching with my neighbour, Clare Paling, you will remember my mentioning her before, one was glad to be able to lend a bit of moral support, her husband being away at the time. It is a refreshing change after some of my parishioners to come across a woman who . . .

Dear mother, Last night I saw a child dying and now I can think of nothing else. I have sat in Mrs Paling's house which I have many times visited in the imagination, and the experience meant nothing at all.

Clare came back into the room and sat down in the armchair. She took a gulp of her drink.

'You thought,' he said, 'at first, that it was . . .'

'Thomas. Yes.'

They sat in silence. She finished her drink and poured another. 'More?' He shook his head.

'Have you ever played roulette?' said Clare.

He looked at her, startled.

'We did once, on some French holiday. I've never been so bored in my life. The only game I've ever found of any interest is chess, and even that palled after a bit.'

He saw, he supposed, what she was on about. He nodded. She said, 'Don't you find it pretty difficult to live with?'

He licked his lips. 'It?'

'Blind fate. The blindness of fate. Or whatever.'

'I suppose,' he began cautiously, 'one has always hoped somehow to come to terms . . .'

'Come to terms is what one never does. Oh, I'm sorry. I didn't mean to snap. That's just what I didn't mean to do. I feel a bit unhinged today.'

He stared at the floor. Boards. Grainy, nicely polished. 'And of course with faith . . .' He stopped. Faith?

'Does it,' she said, 'actually, really, practically – help?'

He scanned the boards; there was a blue thread caught on a splinter. She was asking him a question; she wanted an answer, genuinely wanted. If he looked up she would be staring at him with those grey, rather cold eyes. Yesterday he had seen stark terror in those eyes,

He had wondered, sometimes, about children; looking at the faces of those who have them. Love, the other love, you saw at the cinema, or walking the streets, aged twenty, arm in arm. There wasn't anybody in the world, including his mother, whose death would have caused him more than a momentary regret.

Yet last night he had roved from sleeplessness to nightmare.

The floorboards were offering no help. He looked up. 'I've seen people, occasionally, sometimes the very old, a sort of calm . . .'

'What,' she said, 'about you?'

And of course, his mother used to say, it's a wonderful thing, it'll always be a comfort to you, you'll have something to fall back on that others don't. The stipend's not much, but there it is.

He searched. He travelled from one grey moment to another, examining. Grey, though, they had been, rather than black. Disappointment, disillusion, disenchantment. Eventually he began, cautiously. 'When I was at school I used to want to be Manners, the captain of cricket.' At this point, normally, there would come that snorty laugh; it didn't, for some reason; she was listening to him, not bored – attentive. 'I used to lie in bed at night and will myself to turn into Manners. I used to tell myself stories in which I was Manners. He was tall, that kind of hair that goes over one eye, I don't remember ever speaking to him, even the masters used to kow-tow to him, the younger ones. I knew I wasn't ever going to be Manners, not really, or even anyone like Manners, but it made it more possible to put up with not being him, or like him, to go on thinking like that. At night.' He paused. The glass of sherry was almost empty; he finished it.

'Yes?' said Clare Paling. 'And later?'

He studied the flower picture above the mantelpiece; the flowers became the faces of various girls, girls until this moment almost forgotten, girls quite unlike Mrs Paling, girls who had not, at one time or another . . . Girls who also, at night, had been quite otherwise.

No, he could not go into that.

'I have never,' he went on, 'been ill. Or in any danger. It has been a question more of what hasn't happened. I suppose going on believing it might sometime be different has helped.'

'That's not faith,' said Clare. 'That's hope.'

He had never had a conversation like this before; he was filled with unease.

' "And now abideth faith, hope, charity; these three," ' she said. ' "And the greatest of these . . ." Only you will insist on calling it love, which is not the same.'

'I . . .?'

'Not you personally. Sorry. That repellent new Bible. Charity,' she went on, 'is what I'm a bit short on, I've always considered.' She was silent for a moment. 'Tolerance and generosity and understanding.'

He did not hear her. He thought about words. Hope? There was an old woman in his congregation, a woman in always the same dun-coloured coat and hat, always in the same seat, always present; dour, unapproachable. Was it for words that she was there? He looked up at Clare Paling, sitting in her light, bright sitting-room with books all over her walls and a glass in her hand; he felt a stir of that old confused hostility, a

165

little rush of bile. He said 'Oh, it's all so simple for people like you, you've got an answer to everything. You don't believe in God and you know exactly why you don't believe. The sort of people I know, just ordinary people who come to church, mostly they haven't much idea of why they do believe and I've never been able to tell them because to begin with I wasn't all that clear myself and then . . .' He paused and looked away. 'But you – you go into the church and all you see is carvings and different kinds of windows, you might as well be in an art gallery. Or a museum. There's more to it than that.'

'I know ,' she said.

The bile had subsided. Why wasn't she answering back? She sat there, instead, staring into her glass.

'And words . . .'

She looked up. 'Words I must insist on. Sorry. I didn't want to do battle, though. Not today.'

There was a smell of food. Nice food. He wasn't at all hungry. He had a curious sense of displacement, as though none of this were real. The first time he went abroad, as a young man, he had felt that, continuously.

Clare said 'The trouble with people like me, one of the many troubles, is not so much that we've got all the answers as that we are incapable of suspending disbelief. Not just religious disbelief, either. It's not entirely comfortable, I promise you. In fact often it isn't comfortable at all. This probably isn't very coherent – I shouldn't drink gin in the middle of the day. We try to make sense of the world, and it doesn't make sense, so we take it out on all those other explanations that we find unsatisfactory. And we pile up guilt. Guilt for not having suffered and guilt for being intemperate and uncharitable and' – she looked out of the window at the Green, aqueous in misty rain – 'guilt today because my child is alive and someone else's isn't.'

She stared across the room at him, across the polished floor and the oblong of hairy brightly-coloured rug. 'I must have seemed pretty nasty sometimes. To you. I'm sorry.'

166

George considered. In his present state of unreality such a remark could only be taken on its merits. He said, 'Not particularly. You made me feel stupid.' He waited for his spluttering laugh; again it didn't come. 'Not all that many go out of their way to be nice, anyway.'

Clare blinked. There was an odd look about her, he thought, slightly dilated, as though for her too the occasion was in some way detached from ordinary existence. She got up. 'Would you like another sherry?'

He nodded. She brought the bottle across, poured into his glass. A little spilled onto the floor. She knelt down beside him, mopping with a tissue. She tilted against his legs: her flat bony thighs, the pointed breasts under the thin jersey, the fingers with long clean nails. She sat back, screwing the tissue into a ball. She turned and looked straight at him. 'If there's anything you would like,' she said. 'If there's anything I can do, I think just at this moment I'd rather like you to say. It would be all right.'

He stared at her. A grinning face in the east window of the church; nights of promise, of conjecture. He waited for someone he was not to reply, to act.

'No, thank you,' he said sadly.

He got up. 'I think if you don't mind I'll get back. I'm not that hungry, and there's someone due to telephone about moving the screen for restoration. I hope you don't think I'm being rude.'

Clare Paling rose. She stood with her back to the mantelpiece. 'I don't think you're being rude in the least.'

George went out of her front gate and round into his own. He walked up the patchy green-invaded gravel of the vicarage path and in at the front door. There were five circulars on the mat and a letter from his mother. He picked them up and went into the study. He sat at the desk and entered two christenings and a wedding in the church diary. He made a list of people to be thanked for their endeavours of the previous day.

He looked up. It had stopped raining. The plastic bunting

along the forecourt of the Amoco garage dripped onto the tarmac. The road gleamed with puddles, a trembling reflection of sky and leaves. The church, the gold of its stone all darkened by damp, sat hunched among the churchyard trees. George picked up the report of the church restoration expert and began to read his proposal to include cleaning of the Doom painting in the general reparations, an expensive and tricky job, evidently, but one which, the expert felt, would bring out the colours and greatly enhance the effect.